MW01204407

Just One Taste

THE BILLIONAIRE BARONS OF TEXAS ⤙ BOOK FIVE

CHRIS KENISTON

Indie House Publishing

Indie House Publishing

CHAPTER ONE

"**F**ind anything today you didn't see yesterday?"

When Paige Baron took over the family's interest in a large but failing Texas winery, the best part of the whole deal was Clay, the manager. Bless his heart, he'd done his best to hold the vineyard together for the former owners, but without the proper support, there hadn't been a chance in hell that he'd be able to keep up, never mind prosper.

"Maybe," she muttered, giving herself another moment to be sure.

"Do tell?" A man of few words, Clay was as old as the dirt beneath her feet, but worked harder than any two men half his age. Maybe three.

"I'm thinking it's time." She'd been staring at a barren strip of land adjacent to Baron property. Shortly after Baron Enterprises had purchased the old vineyard, Paige had been approached by a neighbor looking to make a killing on land no one else wanted. Being a woman, too many made the mistake of thinking she was a pushover. But more important than her gender, she was a Baron. Good business instincts were part of her gene pool. On the other hand, her ability to negotiate came from years of watching her older brothers wheel and deal the family's fortune from something already impressive into something bordering on obscene.

It had taken a good deal of playing cat and mouse with the arrogant neighbor, but in the end, they'd agreed on a price less outrageous and very reasonable. Every year as she implemented the next stage in her five year plan, she'd survey the land and think, not yet. This morning, when she stood on the veranda outside the new pavilion, her gut shouted at her for the first time. Dragging her gaze away from the untouched land, she looked to the guy who had been her right hand man since day one. "It's been three years."

Clay nodded at her. There was no need for her to explain, he knew she was talking about her prize hybrid grape. Or what she hoped would become an award winning new blend for the Baron Winery.

In her mind's eye she could see the bare acreage covered with rows of delicious plump grapes waiting to be turned into a fine wine. "We could do a limited edition." That was another thought that had been kicking around in the back of her mind as she considered the wine.

His gaze had drifted to the bare rolling hills. "We could."

Some days, she really hated that male tendency to barely utter a word. "Or?"

"No *or*." He shook his head and turned once again to face her. "It's a good plan."

That's what she wanted to hear. She trusted her gut more than anything, but a word of encouragement from Clay went a long way when it came to keeping her eye on the prize. "We've got multiple new bookings coming up for rather large weddings."

"Miss Eve's was a beautiful party." The older man hadn't known her sister for much longer than he'd known Paige, but he'd taken a shine to the whole family.

"I think there will be enough in the coffers to plant the new grapes."

"The French grape?"

She bobbed her head. Years of traveling the French countryside had brought her in contact with a good many vintners. Some more friendly than others. A few, fearing no competition from the young American female, shared their secrets. One in particular, an aging man who made her grandfather look like a spring chicken, and who swore Paige was the spitting image of his long deceased daughter, promised her when the time was right she could bring his cuttings stateside. If all went as she hoped, in a few more years she'd have sturdy vines and then, given a little more time, she could present the world with a new stellar Baron blend. The mere thought gave her goose bumps.

"You very busy?" The Governor's voice boomed strongly over her shoulder.

Paige swung around and took a few steps forward, enveloping her grandfather in a hug much the way she'd done since she was a little girl. "I've always got time for you."

The old man beamed. "Good. If I could have a few minutes of your time."

Clay cleared his throat. "I need to check on the new girl in the tasting room."

The former governor of the great state of Texas sidled up beside Paige. "Rumor has it the Comets are looking to move their franchise."

Her gaze narrowed as she quickly shifted her thoughts from wine to sports, taking a moment longer to place the name. "Hockey."

"Yes. NHL." The older man dipped his chin slightly. "We've been working on bringing a farm team to Houston, but if we could land the Comets…"

His words drifted off but Paige could see the twinkle in her grandfather's eyes. She'd heard many a story of his childhood, spending winter breaks with all his cousins at his grandfather's home in Colorado. Playing ice hockey on the lake had been one of his fondest memories. No doubt her grandfather could see a Zamboni clearing the ice of their under used stadium in anticipation of a Stanley Cup game as clearly as she could see currently fallow land lined with lush grapes. Her grandfather was a visionary in many ways. He fought hard for his state for many years, and continued to do so for his city, county and state wherever time and money allowed.

"Convincing the northern yankee owners that the Gulf Coast is the perfect spot for relocation won't be easy."

"Money talks." It was one of the first things she'd learned as a Baron. The second thing she'd learned was to use the Baron money for the greater good. Not always an easy task.

"I understand that Daniel Dupree is heading the initial vetting committee."

"The name sounds familiar." She couldn't quite put her finger on it.

"Canadian, played for the Bruins, then the Comets. MVP goalie three Stanley Cups in a row. His career was sidelined when a car accident crushed one leg. They saved the leg, but not his career."

Of course. "He and his brother used to play on the same team. Mitch was probably their biggest fan."

The Governor nodded. "It's my understanding that Dupree is personally visiting the competing cities."

"Is Houston one of them?"

"We're working on it."

Thoughts danced around in her head but none explained why her grandfather was sharing this with her of all people. She knew wine, not hockey.

Her grandfather rolled back on his heels and blew out a soft breath. "One thing I've learned in my life, politically correct or not—a woman in the room helps keep hot-headed men civil."

"Maybe."

"No maybe about it. Eve can't participate and Siobhan's off taking photos of African elephants. Can I count on your help?"

They could put all she knew about ice hockey in the proverbial thimble, but if her grandfather thought she could help... "Absolutely."

Ten cities and now Houston. It had taken Daniel the better part of the last few weeks to eliminate a slew of cities from the running and narrow it down to the best town, now eleven. Most had lofty ambitions without the financial backing his team wanted. As much as he disliked adding another city to his list instead of culling it, the last minute proposal from Houston had everything the team was looking for. Including an already built stadium, a little small, but suitable for ice hockey. No need to haggle with communities and bond proposals to bring the team in. Still, somehow his inclination remained geared toward a cold weather state without an annual hurricane season, like Utah or Wyoming. Utah being the only one of the two on the shorter list. Unfortunately, Wyoming was out. Making the math work for a state that had more antelope than people simply didn't compute.

An existing unused stadium wasn't the only thing Houston had in its favor. Daniel had to admit the idea of an in state rivalry between two hockey teams mirroring the profitable rivalry between the two Pennsylvania teams piqued his interest. The revenue possibilities were enough to make a man drool. On the other hand, the lack of fans in recent games only bolstered the idea that the South was no place for multiple hockey franchises. Maybe.

"You ready?" Kevin, Daniel's right hand on this project, stood in the doorway.

Daniel glanced at his wrist watch. The flight to Utah left in a little under four hours. Just enough time to get to the airport and hurry up to stand in line and weed his way through security. "As ready as I'll ever be."

Kevin slid a piece of paper onto Daniel's desk. "This just came in. New Mexico is withdrawing the bid."

Looking at the sheet in front of him, Daniel bobbed his head. "Wonder who changed their mind?"

"No clue."

From the beginning Daniel wondered how the heck a state with only a few million people wound up on the list. All he could conclude is that someone in New Mexico had extraordinarily deep pockets. Now he wondered what made them change their mind and lock up their bank account.

"Do you have the data for the new addition?"

It took him a few moments to realize that Kevin was referring to Houston and not some other city the owners were thrusting upon him. "All I know is that Governor Baron is one of the backers. Which probably explains why

Houston is the only bidder coughing up the cost of a five star hotel."

"Surely Texas isn't the only one with deep pockets."

Daniel shrugged. "No, but they do say everything is bigger in Texas. It will be interesting to see what they have planned."

"I wonder if they're going to pick you up in one of those stretch limos with cow horns on the grill?"

"Unlikely. I'm renting a car. Besides, I'm pretty sure the horns are only from bulls."

"Nope. The longhorn cattle all have horns. No chauvinism among those bovines."

Daniel chuckled. "Noted." Though why his assistant from Brooklyn knew anything about Texas cattle was beyond him.

"Want some aspirin?"

Not till Kevin asked did Daniel realize he'd been rubbing his knee. When the drunken idiot who ran the red light smashed into the driver side of his car and sent it flying across the intersection into a lamppost, he thought his life was coming to an end. Thanks to a top notch trauma team and his brilliant surgeon, his life was saved, but not his career. After all these years, rubbing away the discomfort in his left leg was so common place, he didn't even realize that his leg had been bothering him. At least not till Kevin went into mother hen mode. For a guy, he was pretty good at noticing little things. "Nah, it's nothing."

His assistant didn't say another word about his leg, merely handed him a fat envelope with all the basic data for every city. Daniel had it all on his laptop, but on plane rides, he preferred to study the information on old fashioned paper instead of a backlit screen. His first assignment was to learn all about the former governor, the committee, the city, and anything that would help him get through this visit sooner than later. Someone may have convinced the committee to allot more days in Houston than any other city on the list, but as far as he was concerned, the quicker he could race through this visit the better. Shaking his head, he stuffed the envelope into his briefcase. How the heck did anyone expect to successfully mix ice hockey and a million degree heat nine months of the year? Despite the lure of the in state rivalry, he was pretty sure he'd already made up his mind. The team needed a cold weather climate where hockey was in the city's blood. There was no way Houston had enough people to create a buzz around hockey. He seriously doubted that the sprawling city would hold any interesting surprises for him. Nope, Houston would definitely be a waste of his time.

CHAPTER TWO

Kevin had been right. Well, partly. When Daniel's plane landed in Houston, a chauffeur and limousine had indeed greeted him, but the vehicle hadn't had horns on the front. He wasn't completely sure if he was relieved or disappointed.

What Daniel had wanted very much to do was decline the ride and find his way to the nearest rental agency for a modest sedan to drive to the meeting, as planned. But his mother's voice in the back of his head reminding him to be gracious and respectful of the efforts of others had him climbing into the luxury leather backseat and taking the opportunity to study his new surroundings. It was no surprise that Houston was one of the largest cities in the country. The freeways were massive, intertwining, and crowded despite it not being anywhere near rush hour.

At the arena, a group of men waited for him. Lined up at the door like staff in a turn of the century British historical, this was the largest delegation he'd encountered so far. There was no doubt that Houston wanted the Comets, even if Daniel wasn't convinced they belonged here. He braced himself for the onslaught of ideas, offers, and even pampering and enticements that would occur.

Immediately, he recognized the former governor standing front and center, and of course his son the senator was another recognizable face in the crowd. The rest of the group, he was able to put a few faces to the names, but most he wasn't sure who they were until introductions were made and handshakes exchanged. Considering the number of Barons involved, he already had a better understanding of just how badly the former governor wanted this team for his state.

"Let's give you a tour of the facility as it currently is. We're open to making any changes you might suggest," the Governor boomed as he clacked his cane along the cement floor, taking the lead during the tour.

The lights were already on when they entered. The arena was prepped with fresh ice, something that must have cost the city, or the Barons, a pretty penny considering they didn't have a team to play on it. As always, the sight of a clean sheet of ice made him itch to put on a pair of skates, grab a sturdy stick, and have a little one on one with a hockey puck. Unfortunately, his sore knee reminded him that even if he could manage a few spins around the rink on ice, there would be no handling of a stick and no chasing pucks. His hockey days were well behind him. Some days that was harder to accept than others, but at least he was still involved with the game he loved, even if it was behind a desk and not holding a stick. Glancing around, most of the older business members of Houston, despite their smiling enthusiasm, didn't look like they had a clue how to lace up. Though the way the senator stared off into the distance, he wondered if this was the Baron who loved the game enough to go to all this trouble, or if a different trouble was on his mind.

"How many seats?" Daniel knew the answer because that was his job, but he wanted to sus out what the Governor would say in his sales pitch.

"For ice hockey, the arena seats 17,000. We can convert the venue for concerts to fit 10,000, but that probably isn't why you're here."

No, Daniel wasn't interested in a Taylor Swift concert. To his surprise, the vibe of the place felt oddly right. He glanced at the now silent scoreboard. He could almost hear the screaming fans, the blow of the referee's whistle, and the sound of racing players battling for control of the puck and slamming against the boards. Still, ice hockey was a cold-weather sport with cold weather fans who'd grown up playing on ponds and lakes all winter long. Houston had not seen ice cold weather in, well, ever.

"What is the venue used for currently?" Daniel eyed the empty seats.

"Since the Aeros left, mostly just concerts," Senator Baron said.

"We do have a junior hockey league. It's new, but there's a large fan base of northern transplants who want their kids to learn the sport they love and will be ready to support the new team when they come," Chase Baron said.

Daniel suppressed a smile that the younger Baron had said "when" not "if."

Another gray haired gentleman whose name Daniel had already forgotten, a city councilmen if he remembered correctly, made a sweeping gesture across the stands. "Of course, the community's tax dollars as well as private funding as laid out in our proposal are available immediately to use as you see fit."

Governor Baron pointed past the ice. "You'll want to see what we've done to the locker rooms. They were state of the art when the former hockey team played here, but we thought your team would appreciate some upgrades. Of course we are open to make any changes or additional improvements you think necessary to accommodate the players."

The home team locker room sported everything necessary for a hockey team and then some.

"We have started interviewing yoga instructors and massage therapists. We'll be ready to sign contracts with them as soon as you say the word." Governor Baron smiled confidently.

They were doing a full-court press, or in this case, a full-rink press. He couldn't help being amused. Having been to all but two of the other cities on his list before Houston, and even though they'd all done their utmost to put their best foot forward, the old saying was proving accurate— everything *is* bigger in Texas. The committee seemed confident the decision would be made on the spot. It wouldn't surprise him to find himself later in the day in a tasteful man cave somewhere filled with cigar smoke and drinking scotch with the committee expecting to seal the deal.

Clearly, they were committed to the Comets' move and that was a check in the plus column for Houston. He liked everything he'd seen so far, but things weren't as easy as these men were making it out to be. He'd been around the block enough times to know, nothing goes as smoothly as these people were making it out to be.

When the tour ended, Daniel shook hands again. The Governor put his hand on Daniel's shoulder. "Do you have any questions?"

"Not at the moment, but there's still much to review." For one thing, he needed to rent a car and check out the city for himself.

"Excellent. In the papers the committee sent you there is a tentative schedule for your stay. From here you've got some time to settle in at your hotel and then we will pick you up to escort you to Baron Cellars. We thought you might enjoy a personal tour and chance to sample the fine wines of Texas. You'll find Houston has much to offer."

Somehow, he hadn't doubted that even if Houston didn't have much of interest, the Governor would find something. He also wondered if wine was the opening act and scotch and cigars would come later? Of course, there was only one way to find out. Though a small part of him wished the Baron's owned a brewery instead of a winery, he couldn't help but be intrigued. Just how much *did* Houston have to offer?

Climbing ladders was probably Paige's least favorite thing to do but she'd assigned everyone else other tasks. Of course the stupid bulb a good twelve feet high would pick this morning to burn out. She had enough on her plate getting ready for the upcoming wine competition, now she had to deal with a visiting hockey VIP *and* changing this dumb light before the Governor and his entourage arrived.

With only a few minutes before anyone would enter the tasting room, she quickly set up the A frame ladder and with a bulb in her hand climbed higher than she liked. If her brothers knew how much she disliked heights, they'd never let her hear the end of it. The adrenaline junky gene that even Siobhan seemed to have inherited, clearly skipped over her. Standing on a two foot step stool was the extent of her comfort zone.

Reaching the highest step, she actually said a short prayer. How her siblings bungee jumped, climbed mountains, drove at the near speed of light—and enjoyed it—she'd never understand. Stretching to unscrew the bulb, the squeak of the door hinge had her adding one more thing to her mental to-do list. Oil that hinge. The winery had to be perfect down to the very last hinge when the competition committee came by. The second thought to cross her mind had her eyes popping open wide and gripping the top shelf of the ladder. If the door was opening, and she was in front of the door…

Sure enough, the next sound to send shivers up her spine was the thud of the door against the ladder about two seconds before the aluminum structure wobbled beneath her feet, rattling her like a rag doll in the grips of an angry dog. "Oh, sh…" escaped her lips at the same time a decidedly male voice completed words that she hadn't dared finish.

A strong, hot, and most definitely masculine hand landed splat against the small of her back. His other hand must have gripped the ladder as she couldn't see any other reason the thing hadn't tipped over, hurling her through the air.

"I'm sorry." The deep timbre of the man's voice did little to assuage the panic still coursing through her veins.

Blowing out a deep breath, she sucked in another slow one, forcing her heart to stop pounding like a woodpecker against a favorite tree. The ladder gave one last wiggle before settling sturdily in place again, giving her a moment to regroup, her heart still pounding like a bass drum in her chest.

She'd almost forgotten the strong hand and the male

voice until he cleared his throat and slid his hand away from her back. Still breathing deeply, she looked down into eyes so blue they might have been carved from the sky. She blinked and the man smiled.

"I'm sorry. I didn't see the ladder when I barged in here." He took a slow step in retreat. "Are you okay?"

"I'm fine. Accidents happen. This wasn't your fault."

His gaze darted from the base of the ladder to the door then back to her. "Well, I think it is. Can I help you with that?" He indicated the bulb still in her hand.

It was a miracle in the shaky moment that she hadn't dropped it. Still, she would sooner let a guest pour himself a glass of wine than have one change a light bulb. "I'm good. Let me fix this and I'll move the ladder." She motioned her head in the direction of the opposite side of the room. "The bar is that way."

"How about I hang onto this in case anyone else comes in? I'm expecting some other people to meet me here."

Glancing down at the crop of thick blond hair that dipped over his brow, shading those beautiful baby blue eyes, her mind wandered to how pale strands reflected the sunlight from the nearest window. Not till he cleared his throat once again, did she remember he'd asked her to let him help. "Oh. Yes, that's a good idea. Thank you."

Letting the guests help was not in her nature, but having someone else plow through the doorway and send her flying across the room was an even less appealing option. Moving quickly so she could get back to solid ground, she changed the bulb and climbed down the ladder.

Just then Clay entered the tasting room, glanced over at her and the ladder and shook his head. "I could have done that."

"It only took a minute." She smiled at the older man.

"At least let me put that away for you." It wasn't a question. The manager already had the thing folded and out of the way.

"Thanks, Clay." Paige turned to the customer. "Can I interest you in a glass of wine, a quick tasting, or would you rather wait for your friends?"

The man didn't get a chance to answer because her grandfather and her brother waltzed into her tasting room. Sporting huge smiles, the two men in her family strolled directly to the gentleman's side. Which could only mean one thing, the man who had both almost knocked her off her feet and saved her backside at the same time, must be the hockey player they were wooing. *Marvy.*

She pasted on her customer service smile and bobbed her head at her grandfather. "Governor."

The old man winked at her. The small gesture was the former military man's way of giving her silent reassurance. "I see you've met Daniel."

"Not exactly." Somehow, wobbling at the top of a ladder and almost landing in front of the VIP of the day had not been the way she'd hoped to meet, or impress, her grandfather's guest.

Daniel reached out a hand that engulfed hers. "Daniel Dupree. It's a pleasure."

His touch warmed her to the core and something tingled up her arm. It took a determined effort not to snap her hand back. "Paige Baron. Nice to officially meet you."

"Yes." The corners of his mouth tipped north, bringing an extra sparkle to his eyes. "I really am sorry about that."

Her brother frowned momentarily before putting on his politician's smile. "She's our winemaker extraordinaire."

"I must admit, you didn't look like a custodian." Daniel held onto her for a moment longer, before suddenly blinking as if only now noticing he had not let go, and pulled his hand away.

"Yes, well." She took another step back and waved her arm toward the bar. "Shall we move on until the others arrive?"

"Lead the way, Miss Baron."

That man's smile was doing funny things to Paige's mind. Or maybe it was just the aftershock of almost killing herself changing a stupid light bulb. That had to be it. She took a step forward. "Please, call me Paige."

Daniel nodded at her, and moved in the direction she'd pointed.

Her grandfather fell into step beside her. His voice a barely audible whisper, the Governor winked again. "Atta girl."

The comment almost had her stumbling to a stop. *Atta girl?* Her gaze drifted to the man now a few feet ahead of her, the sun bleached blond hair and crisp fit of his clothes against a well built and well exercised body. All she could think was… *Oh, boy.* The rest of this little effort was either going to be really interesting, or a real fiasco, and danged if she had a clue which would win out.

CHAPTER THREE

aniel knew the next few days were designed to win him over to Houston, but if getting to know Paige Baron a little better was part of the deal, he was all in. The former governor, the senator, the city councilman and Paige were all smiles.

Standing on the veranda staring down at the vineyard, the Governor's cell sounded off and he stared down with a frown.

"Anything wrong, Governor?" A similar buckling of her brows appeared on Paige's face.

"No." The Governor shook his head. "But it looks like I'm not going to be able to join you for dinner after all." The frown slipped and the smile he'd been sporting most of the day reappeared. "Paige, you won't mind stepping in for me, will you?"

The way her gaze darted from him to her brother and grandfather and back, Daniel thought for sure she was going to turn and run. Had he made that poor of an impression? A smile similar to the one her grandfather and brother sported slid into place. "I'd be happy to."

"Good. Good." The Governor tapped his cane. "We have reservations at Kirby's."

Paige nodded and her brother placed his hand on her arm. "Sorry, I can't join you. Time to get back to the day job. My flight to DC leaves in a couple of hours."

Her eyes softened, but her smile remained intact as she patted his arm. "No problem." The genuine affection arcing between the two siblings brought a smile to Daniel's face. The interaction reminded him of his own brother. Thirteen months his junior, his brother Henry and him had been as close as twins. Hockey had been both their passions. The best years of his life had been the two years they'd played on the same team before his accident, but he wasn't going down that particular memory lane.

The Governor slapped him on the back. "I'd say you're in good hands. Do you have all my numbers in case of anything?"

The thought occurred to Daniel, if he called at midnight, the Governor would probably answer and respond to any whim. "I have all of your contact information. Thank you for the winery tour and the welcome to Houston, sir."

The two men shook hands. A few more encouraging words from the Governor to his granddaughter and the three men turned and made their way to the parking lot.

Daniel kept his gaze on the men's backs as they chatted by the cars. "They really want this hockey team."

She leaned against the back bar, studying him. "Doesn't everyone? I mean, all the applicants?"

"They do, but in just a few hours I can see an intent that I haven't noticed yet."

Her smile grew even wider and her eyes twinkled with delight. "They often get what they want."

"Thanks for the warning."

"Just a fact." Her grin remained intact. As a matter of fact, her gaze held a confidence that made him feel as if she knew something he didn't but should. "I won't be easily swayed."

She shrugged and pushed away from the bar. "You never know."

Lifting the glass of wine in front of him, he took a slow sip. "Why don't you tell me more about the wine business."

One of her eyebrows cocked up. "You're interested in wine?"

He was interested in Paige and the wine business came with it. "Anything can be interesting if someone has a passion for it. Anyone with eyes and ears can see you love this place."

"I do. When I landed here I found a home. I mean, I love my condo, and the ranch has always been a favorite place for the whole family to gather, but here..." She waved her arm in a sweeping motion. "The dirt beneath my fingers, the roll of the hills, the perfect alignment of every vine as far as the eye can see, the dew drops on the grapes in the early morning, and then, mixing and mastering the perfect blends of savory wine, all of it feels like a little piece of heaven on earth."

Looking out at the vineyards he could see why she loved it. "You like roses too?"

Paige chuckled. "Yes, but that's not why there's a rose bush at the head of every row. Roses and grapes are vulnerable to the same diseases, but roses aren't as hardy. If the roses are infested then we can treat the grapes before it's a problem."

"I see."

"I learned that trick from the vineyards in France. They all have rose bushes at the lead of the rows." Her gaze drifted off into the distance and heavy silence fell.

"Anything wrong?"

Her head snapped around to face him. "Sorry, just thinking. I have to taste something from one of the tanks. Today is the halfway point of its aging. Would you like to taste it with me?"

"As long as having any clue what I'm tasting isn't a requirement."

That brought out the sincere chuckle he'd hoped for. "Not at all. As a matter of fact, it would be helpful to get a layman's point of view."

He bit back a grin of his own. "I might lead you astray."

She shook her head. "I doubt it. Besides, I wouldn't be a Baron if I weren't willing to take chances. Follow me."

Setting the glass down on the counter, he watched her cross the large room. The question running through his mind now was how much of a chance on Houston was he willing to take?

★

Paige asking Daniel into the tank room had been impulsive. Now that he was here she was second-guessing herself. She wasn't ready to share her projects, so why did she invite this man of all people to taste something only she had ever tasted? Scrawled on each tank was the grape and the date it had been put in the tank. She'd found that to be the best method of identifying each tank's contents because when necessary, she could easily wipe off the markings. He studied each one with an intensity she hadn't expected. Did he know more about grapes and wine than he'd let on? She crooked her finger over her shoulder. "The vintage I want to taste is back here."

The must, or what most people would call the juice, was in a tank in the back. She'd been aging it longer than the rest of her grapes, not wanting to disturb it in the slightest. The other tanks in front of her special efforts could be shuffled around, but this one needed to stay still.

His head tipped to one side as he read one label. "Victoria Red?"

"It grows well in Texas, and is resistant to a lot of diseases. The challenge is that everyone else is growing it as well." She had done everything in her power to change the terroir, the dirt that would nourish her precious vines, in order to bring out different aspects of the grape. She could only do so much. The soil was the soil, but she could change the amount of irrigation.

"So what you're wanting is a way to stand out from the crowd?"

"Exactly."

"Why stainless steel tanks?" His gaze drifted over multiple tanks. "I thought wine was made in barrels."

She pulled two glasses off a shelf and leaned over the spigot for the tank, filling each glass with an ounce of the aging wine. "Because they don't affect the wine as much as other containers. This way I have more control over the taste." She handed him one of the two glasses.

"Then no oak barrels?"

"I have those. I'll also put some of the wine in a traditional barrel to age, but I'm still playing with this.

Figuring out what I can make."

He touched his glass with hers. "To potential."

His choice of words made her smile. Deliberate, yet open ended. Whether he was referring to the possibilities for the wine or a hockey team in Houston, she had no idea. Or maybe he was referring to something all together different. Either way, she had to agree and held her glass to his. "To potential."

Allowing the juice to roll around in her mouth, she slowly gave an almost imperceptible nod. She liked how her new wine coated her tongue the way a Cabernet would.

"What should I be tasting?" he asked.

Swallowing quickly, she shook her head. "Not how it works. You tell me what you taste."

"But I don't know wine."

"Doesn't matter. There are no wrong answers."

"You sure?" One brow lifted higher than the other highlighting the twinkle in his eyes.

"This isn't a test, Daniel. I want to know what you taste. You have no preconceived notions."

He took another sip as she watched. His Adam's apple bobbed up and down as he swallowed. "Cigar, but not the stinky type. Chocolate. I never would have thought those two would go together."

His detailed observation surprised her. He was an astute observer and his palette more mature than she'd expected. She could get to like that in a man. Not that she was in the market for one.

"Tobacco. We put that on the tasting sheet, but it isn't stale cigarettes. It's a fine cigar from Cuba."

His third sip was slower and more thoughtful. "Ganache."

"Ganache?"

"Not a cheap chocolate, but the kind drizzled over a dessert in a fine restaurant."

She smiled and held her glass up to him. "That is exactly the flavor I'm going for."

"Then perhaps we should be toasting to success?" He took another sip, nodding his head. "I like it."

"Good. Here's hoping a lot of other people agree with you." She set her empty glass on the table. "If we're going to make the reservation, we'd better get moving. Kirby's is one of the best restaurants in Houston and very popular at the dinner hour. Even for the Governor, if we're late, the reservation is lost."

"That I find hard to believe, but your wish is my command."

Oh heavens did that last remark send her mind rushing off to places it had no business going. "I'll drive. We can come back for your car later."

"Are you sure it won't be out of the way to come back?"

She shook her head. "I practically live at the winery these days."

"Really?" That same eyebrow shot up.

"Well, maybe that's a slight exaggeration, but between the family ranch and the winery, I'm starting to forget what my condo looks like."

"All work and no play isn't good for a soul." He smiled at her.

"Says the man who used to play for a living." The way the sparkle in his eyes instantly dimmed had her regretting the blunt banter. "Sorry, I didn't mean…"

He shook his head and held up his hand. "No need for apologies. You're right. I did play for a living. A little too much sometimes, but I'm suddenly starved. Shall we go?"

With a nod of her head she fell into step beside him, waved to her manager, and wondered what thoughts had driven the light from this man's eyes? More than that, she wondered why she cared.

CHAPTER FOUR

I n the parking lot, they'd barely stepped out the winery doors when a group of men came strolling up. This late in the day it was unusual to have folks stopping by, but she'd been working on making the winery a destination for more than tourists. The idea had come to her when visiting the Coppola Winery in Sonoma. Tonight's late arrivals gave her hope her efforts were paying off.

They'd made it halfway to her car when one of the guys stopped in his tracks and, his jaw almost touching the concrete muttered, "Daniel Dupree." When Daniel paused, the young man beamed like a kid with a new bike on Christmas. "Holy cow. It really is you!"

"That's what my mother keeps telling me." Daniel reached out to shake the guy's hand. "Nice to meet you."

"I can't believe you're in Houston. This is so cool!"

At first, Paige worried this would make them late for their reservation, then it struck her, an avid hockey fan was a gift from God. This guy's familiarity with Daniel would probably go a lot further to show Daniel that Houston was the right place for the Comets than anything she or her grandfather could do or say. Suppressing a smile, she stood aside and listened to the men chatting hockey and NHL for a few long minutes before they reluctantly bid their farewells and headed into the building.

Meeting celebrities was nothing new for a Baron. Paige had grown up with famous people coming and going. Once she'd even had the chance to attend a gala with her grandfather in honor of the British royal family. What she'd learned from all those encounters was that not everyone with fame or fortune were nice people. Considering all their wealth and influence, she liked thinking the Barons were pretty normal. Watching Daniel interact with the unexpected fans, her opinion of him inched up a degree or two. He had been friendly and polite and truly did not seem the least bit irritated or unsettled by having his evening interrupted. Apparently Daniel was a man that everyone liked. This man was easily growing on her. Truth was, it had been a very long time since she'd been so thoroughly charmed by anyone.

"Sorry about that." Daniel strode beside her. "I hadn't expected to be recognized down here."

"Don't underestimate the hockey fanbase in Texas. The Stars have done very well since moving from Minnesota. The Houston Comets could be Stanley Cup winners too."

Daniel cocked his head, staring at her. "You're a hockey fan?"

"I have four brothers. I have to be able to hold my own with any sport. Though I freely admit hockey isn't my favorite. I much prefer sports like baseball where the players aren't trying to kill each other." Paige stopped at her car.

"We're not trying to kill each other. We're trying to score goals and win games. And the Stanley Cup."

"Not buying it." She clicked the key fob and Daniel opened her door for her. So the man was nice, charming, and a gentleman too. Most days she felt chivalry was a dying concept. Sliding into the driver seat, she waited for Daniel to circle the hood and climb in on the passenger side before turning the ignition. "I have sat center ice and heard the grunts and groans as players are slammed into the boards. And the faces smashed against the plexi-glass." She actually shuddered at the memory. "Definitely trying to kill each other."

To her surprise, Daniel let out a deep chuckle. "I might be willing to agree that it's a rough sport. Heaven knows there are plenty of split lips and loose teeth involved, but no one wants anyone to really get hurt."

She shrugged. "Okay, maybe kill each other is a little strong, but I'd still rather have box seats to a baseball game."

"Noted." He smiled at her.

It didn't take long to get to Kirby's. Though traffic in this part of town was always heavy, for whatever reason tonight, she didn't get stuck in a single bottleneck.

"Nice to see you, Miss Baron." The valet nodded and helped her out of her car. "It's been a while. We're glad to have you back."

"Thank you, Nick. Glad to be back." There was no need for a ticket. Nick had been working the valet station every weekend since his senior year of high school. He knew exactly which car was hers or all of her siblings and cousins. Now that she thought about it... "Aren't you graduating soon?"

His smile grew. "Yes, ma'am. This June. And your brother Chase has offered me a position with Baron Enterprises."

"Tell Chase to treat you right or he'll have to answer to me."

"Yes, ma'am." The young man actually blushed before sliding into the car and easing the vehicle away from the curb.

"Do you know so much about all the valets where you eat?" Daniel fell into step beside her.

"Some." At the door the hostess greeted her with the same enthusiasm that Nick had, though she didn't remember the woman's name. Few people in the restaurant business lasted as many years as Nick had. The hostess seated them in a quiet booth with a nice view of the city lights. "Order anything you like. Everything is good. Kirby's has been one of the best recommended steakhouses in Houston for as long as I can remember."

He nodded, and very slowly perused the menu.

When a pretty waitress came by to take their order, Paige took the liberty of ordering the stuffed mushrooms for an appetizer. "Do you like mushrooms?"

Without lifting his eyes from the menu, he nodded, then as almost an afterthought, looked up and smiled at her. "Yes, I do."

"Great." She ordered the ribeye medium.

"I'll have a baked sweet potato and the sautéed brussels sprouts, no bacon."

The waitress nodded and stared at him silently. When he didn't say anything else, she frowned. "And which steak would you like?"

"None, thank you." He handed her the menu. "Just the potato and brussels sprouts."

Paige's gaze flittered to the stunned waitress and back. Good grief. How had her grandfather not done his homework? Daniel Dupree was a vegetarian.

There was no way for Daniel to hide he was a vegetarian at a steakhouse. There was nothing new about people assuming he ate meat, he was used to it. What he didn't like was the mortified look on Paige's face. "It's fine. I love sweet potatoes."

She shook her head. "We should go somewhere else. I'm sorry, I didn't know. There's a vegan restaurant I've heard—"

Holding his hand up to her, it was his turn to shake his head. "First of all, I'm not vegan. Secondly, this is perfectly fine."

"I don't know."

He could see the hesitation on her face. "They have blueberry cobbler on the menu. One of my favorites."

"Really? Or are you just trying to make me feel better?"

"Honestly, I do want you to feel better." Right now he wanted more than anything for her to like him, though he had no idea why it seemed to matter so much. In a few more days he'd be moving on and probably never see her again. "But, yes, I really do love blueberry cobbler."

She blew out a heavy sigh and then smiled. "In that case, you know what they say. Life is short…"

Through a chuckle, he finished the sentence. "Eat dessert first."

"Shall we?" She raised her brows at him.

With a nod, he waved down the waitress and instructed her to bring two blueberry cobblers before the meal.

She leaned back in her seat. "I'm not sure how the Governor didn't know this. I didn't think the man made mistakes. Ever."

"It's not on my resume or anything. No reason he should know."

The waitress appeared with their desserts, and set the first dish in front of Paige and then gave Daniel his. Instead of the standard question of did they need anything else, she leaned in over the table and lowered her voice. "I've always wanted to order dessert first but never have the nerve. I think I just might do this the next time I eat out. Enjoy your meal."

Daniel dug into his cobbler and almost moaned.

"You really do like blueberry cobbler."

"Don't look so surprised. I told you I did." She had a little dollop of blueberry syrup on her lip and he had a suddenly irresistible urge to reach out and wipe it away. Maybe even steal a kiss. Definitely not a good idea. "It's easy to find peach cobbler or apple, but blueberry is a treat."

"Well, I'm delighted they had it." She stabbed at her dessert with her fork before looking up at him. "But you realize if you move to Texas, you're going to be invited to an awful lot of barbecues. We're known for our briskets."

He shrugged again. "I'll learn to deal. I spent years on road trips dining with guys who could have eaten an entire cow if given the opportunity. A barbecue here or there isn't going to kill me."

"Are you always this easygoing?" She leaned back and took a sip of her water.

"The way I look at it, I can choose to be annoyed and irritated, which will change nothing. Or I can roll with the punches and enjoy the positives. In this case, that would be a nice dinner with you."

"Okay," she chuckled, "easy going *and* charming."

"At your service, ma'am." The wide smile on her face was a sweet reward. What he'd expected to be a boring dinner talking hockey and listening to boasting about what the city had to offer, had turned into a pleasant evening with a beautiful and smart woman. Too bad, despite the possibilities, as far as he was concerned, the franchise needed a home already rooted in ice hockey, which meant Houston wasn't even in the running.

CHAPTER FIVE

The Governor's secretary had emailed Daniel the rest of his itinerary. The email left no room for diverting from the schedule and that was why Daniel was currently driving towards the Baron ranch—Paradise Ridge. Interesting name. He'd have thought for sure a family as powerful and renowned as the Barons would have their own name brazened across the archway to their home.

They were all meeting at the family homestead and then driving to Galveston. Who "all" meant, Daniel wasn't sure. From his research, he'd already learned that Paige had a lot of siblings, but were they all going to be part of today's plans? He'd rather have Paige to himself, spend what little time he had left in Houston uncovering more about this intriguing woman, but today, the show was directed by the Governor.

Various high-end cars were parked neatly in the driveway. A couple almost had Daniel drooling. It took him a moment to remember that one of Paige's brothers is a race car driver. He was guessing the Lamborghini was his. Daniel pulled into an empty spot behind Paige's SUV and took his time strolling past the parked cars. It took every ounce of willpower he possessed not to wander up to the Italian sports car, caress the fender, and beg for the car keys. He'd driven some sweet cars but nothing like this.

Before he could reach for the handle to the main house, the door opened. A man loaded down with beach towels literally up to his eyebrows almost collided with Daniel. The mountain of terrycloth shifted left and a hand snaked out from under the towels. "You must be Daniel. I'm Craig, one of the Governor's many grandsons, and Paige's brother."

"Nice to meet you."

Craig nudged his head in the direction of the doorway. "Paige is inside finishing up breakfast." Craig leaned a little closer. "Don't worry; the whole family won't be joining us on this trip."

Were his thoughts that easy to read? He opted to simply smile, nod and move on. After all, one of the many things his mama had drummed into him from the moment he could talk was that sometimes it was better not to say a word. So intrigued by the cars, Daniel hadn't paid much attention to the stately home until he crossed the threshold.

A butler, at least he assumed by the stoic expression and formal suit that the man standing a few feet inside the doorway was the butler, addressed him. "The family is expecting you. They're in the front parlor."

Yep. The butler. The guy turned on his heel and led the way. Everywhere Daniel's gaze landed, there was one stunning item after another. A few he knew had to be worth more than the cars on the other side of the front door. He'd known that the Barons had money, but this was beyond his wildest expectations. His mind drifted back to Paige's comment yesterday that the Barons usually get what they wanted. Now he understood a little better just how likely that was.

"Daniel, hi," Paige said from a doorway down the long hall. "Come in. You want some coffee for the road?"

"Uh, sure."

She motioned him in her direction so he followed. The large and bright kitchen could have easily been in any design magazine or television show. State of the art equipment, and long slabs of countertop would be a chef's dream. The staff, on the other hand, probably fit in better with a turn of the century British TV saga.

"How do you drink it?" A large silver coffee pot in hand, Paige glanced up at him.

"One sugar is fine." Daniel watched intently as she poured the hot liquid into a massive travel mug. Somehow the plastic container seemed horribly out of place in the pristine kitchen and what he suspected was a sterling coffee pot.

A strong hand slapped Daniel on the back and he looked into the Governor's face. The casual attire surprised him. His starched shorts with perfect creases down the front reminded Daniel the older man was also former military. The short sleeve Hawaiian shirt and leather sandals offset the starched shorts. The man looked ready for a day at the beach. The itinerary only said a drive to Galveston. He assumed for a tour of the old town and popular restaurants. Actually spending the day on the beach hadn't occurred to him. Daniel had dressed down, but not to the point of sitting on a sandy beach.

"Good morning." Mrs. Baron sidled up beside the Governor. "I see Paige is setting you up with coffee."

"Grams, this is Daniel. Daniel, my grandmother, Lila Baron."

"It's a pleasure." As his mom had taught him, he waited for the woman to extend her hand before shaking it. He might not have had the wealth and breeding that the Barons had, but his parents were firm believers in good old fashioned manners too.

Just then two rambunctious furballs came barreling down the hall and through the doorway. All Lila Baron had to do was clear her throat and the two pups immediately came to a skidding halt at her feet and plopped their bottoms down to look up at her. Even though they were statue still, the furry tails were swishing back and forth like windshield wipers on a stormy day.

"Much better," she addressed the pups, leaning over to scratch each one behind the ears before straightening and turning to Daniel. "If you're hungry, Hazel made extra sausage croissant breakfast sandwiches. They're better than the word sandwich implies."

"Thank you, ma'am, maybe another time."

Paige handed Daniel the travel mug. "We have a few minutes before we leave, follow me and I'll give you the quick patio tour."

Daniel nodded at the Governor and his wife, then followed Paige outdoors. He didn't know which was more impressive, the patio suitable for a royal summer home, or the view of blankets of rolling hills at the feet of the tiled steps.

It made perfect sense the Barons would have a showcase ranch. They probably had enough petty cash lying around to buy a ranch, a fleet of cars, a hockey team, or pretty much anything they set their heart on. Right now there was no doubt their hearts were set on the Comets in Houston. There was also little doubt that it had nothing to do with making more money. They had enough.

A different door than they'd come through from the kitchen opened. "Ready to get on the road?"

Paige turned. "We're ready, sir." Looking back at Daniel, she smiled. "You can ride with me. Craig will drive Grams and the Governor."

"Lead the way." He waved an arm toward the house, and going through still another door, he followed Paige past a wall of family portraits he assumed were Barons of yesteryear. Out the front door, he glanced over his shoulder at the Baron home. From the outside the house reminded him of Tara, the plantation in *Gone with the Wind*. From the inside, he could easily be in any of the castles of the British royal family. Neither of which made sense in ranch country, and yet, somehow, it all seemed to work. Circling around the hood of the SUV, Daniel held the door for Paige and then closed it behind her. As he trotted back to the passenger side, he caught a glimpse of the Governor still at the top of the front steps watching him.

Something in the way the man spied him gave Daniel the feeling he'd just passed a test he hadn't known he was taking. Which begged the question, what else did this man have in store for him?

Conversation on the drive to Galveston bounced from one

topic to another. Paige couldn't remember the last time she'd spent time with someone who could talk about anything from the challenges of the increase in new Doodle breeds to the expected rise in society of centenarians. Not at all what she expected from a former professional jock, but it certainly had made the drive to Galveston all the more pleasant.

She was practically spitting with laughter as they entered the parking lot to the marina and he finished up a story on the pitfalls of getting caught sneaking out after curfew in the middle of Stanley Cup playoffs. "Needless to say, we were all in the team office when we returned from that trip."

"How much trouble did you get into?" Paige parked her SUV.

"Depends how you define trouble. Since we made it to the finals, we weren't suspended from playing, but let's just say we lost a few privileges on the next road trip."

As he'd done the other day, he quickly opened Paige's door and extended his hand to help her out of the car. Not able to remember the last time she'd gone on a date and had the guy hurry to open doors, pull out chairs, and extend a helping hand, she couldn't help think maybe she'd been dating all the wrong men. Of course, Daniel wasn't exactly a date. Despite her grandfather's wish to have her assistance in swaying the former hockey player to choose Houston, this entire escapade was little more than a means to an end. When the next few days were over, the good looking team scout would be moving on. On the other hand, there was nothing in her grandfather's playbook that said until all was said and done, that she couldn't simply sit back and enjoy the man's company.

Dragging her thoughts back to the conversation about daring team escapades and rebellious youth, she stepped onto the blacktop and nodded a silent thank you for the help. "Aren't team dinners supposed to be a bonding moment?"

"They are, but the team looks forward to the laid back, no real rules social time, so our bosses succeeded in making sure we never pulled a stunt like that again." He opened her back door and pulled out the bag she'd set on the rear seat.

"I can take that." She held out her hand.

A twinkle in his eye and lopsided grin teasing his lips, Daniel slowly shook his head. "My mama would roll over in her grave if I let you carry this."

Knowing when to stand her ground and when to accept defeat, she bobbed her head and waved her arm at the yacht everyone in the family loved. "Mostly my brother Kyle uses this as his home away from home, but whenever she's in port, the family gathers for fun in the sun and wind."

His stance a little stiff, he slowly nodded before following her. "I didn't realize when the itinerary said Galveston that we were going to be on a boat. Isn't this hurricane season?"

"Technically, the season started last month, but the weather is perfect, with no high winds or storms in the forecast for days. No better way to enjoy the gulf coast than on the Baroness."

"I see."

She wished he'd sounded a tad more enthusiastic. The family needed him to enjoy every minute of his stay. If he liked the ship, the water, and the city, he should be more inclined to choose Houston for his team. Though she wouldn't mind if he liked her too, at least a little. But for now, the true objective of this little excursion was to show Daniel a good time.

The tension in his stride gave her the sense that she was going to have to work harder to sell this trip to Daniel. That was okay. She was up to the task.

Reaching the end of the pier, his steps slowed, and his eyes widened as he scanned the ship from bow to stern, then let out a whistle. "That's beautiful."

She couldn't help the grin that took over her face. This was more of the reaction she'd been hoping for. "If you haven't figured it out, we Barons don't do anything halfway."

Daniel laughed. "Apparently not."

"Come on. I'll show you around. The crew will be

ready to get underway as soon as the Governor boards."

Daniel's gaze darted back and forth across the ship before he forced a stiff smile and followed her aboard. Something was off but she didn't have a clue what she was doing wrong. Whatever it was, she'd better figure it out fast.

Every moment of each day he was realizing more and more that the Barons had more than enough money to finance their own team. Why the heck did they want his?

"Welcome aboard the Baroness." The brother with the stack of towels in his arms from the house stood grinning at him like the Cheshire Cat.

"Permission to come aboard." He'd seen enough movies to know a person is supposed to ask to come aboard.

"Granted." Craig smiled. "But I should warn you, I'm not the captain."

He chuckled and feeling solid flooring beneath his feet, relaxed. "I won't hold that against you."

"Wish more people felt that way." The man laughed heartily.

Every inch of this family yacht shouted sheer decadence and yet Daniel had never felt more at home. The soft leather seating in the room they'd all gathered in was more inviting than off putting. The shiny brass and polished wood warmed the large space. What was it they said—everything is bigger in Texas. He was sure he was barely beginning to understand the truth of the old cliché. Laughter carried from the opposite direction and he realized more of the family was already onboard. He didn't know what he had expected from today, but this was for sure not it.

"Everyone here?" The Governor appeared from yet another doorway. Daniel couldn't imagine how many rooms this *little* yacht had.

"All aboard and accounted for." A bright eyed young woman with light auburn hair grinned at the old man.

"That's my sister Siobhan. Her trip overseas was cut

short and she surprised us this morning." Paige whispered at his side. The sudden realization of how close she stood by him warmed his senses. Taking a step back, he resisted the urge to literally shake the feeling off.

The bright eyed sibling approached and shook his hand. One by one the people in the room he had yet to meet came up to him, everyone smiling as they made polite introductions. A few of the men slapped backs and teased each other about things that only they understood, the playful attitudes adding to the comfort of the room.

"Care for a drink?" the Governor asked.

"Just water, thank you."

Paige nodded. "One water coming up."

He watched her cross the room, or was it considered a cabin? On a ship like this, cabin simply didn't fit. A few more seconds passed and she handed him the glass. A tall, slender man in a white jacket balanced a large tray of hors d'ouevres on one hand, offering the morsels to each guest before leaving the remainder on a massive driftwood table in the center of the room.

Just as he reached for a mini quiche, a flutter of movement rolled in his gut. His eyes lifted to the massive wall of windows and his brain connected the dots. They were moving. He waited a moment, a sense of dread filling him. Another minute and his stomach settled and his shoulders relaxed. All would be well. Popping the bite sized appetizer into his mouth, he almost groaned with delight.

"How are they?" Paige asked.

He reached for another. "Delicious."

"They're a favorite. The cook at the ranch has tried to copy the recipe but they never come out the same and the ship's chef, Howard, won't share."

Daniel popped another one in his mouth. They really were delicious. Suddenly the boards under his feet seemed less secure. Glancing up at the windows he realized they were moving more quickly. Too quickly. The mushrooms in his stomach seemed to have taken up boxing. *Uh oh.*

A look of sheer panic flashed in Paige's eyes, and her hand settled on his arm. "Is there a problem?"

He started to shake his head and immediately regretted the movement. There was definitely a problem. "I get seasick."

CHAPTER SIX

Had Paige personally prepared and hand-fed Daniel salmonella-spoiled appetizers, she couldn't have felt worse. The man turned green and she momentarily froze. His reaction was not anywhere on her radar. It simply had never occurred to her to ask if he liked sailing. Everyone loved the Baroness, and no one ever got seasick. Until now. Sticking her arm straight out with one finger pointing at the exit, she barked, "Out on the deck."

Her hand gently against his back, she nudged him toward the closest door. Even though she knew being seasick had something to do with what the inner ear was sensing and what the eyes were seeing, she was pretty sure fresh salt air should help. At least she sure hoped so.

Leaning against the railing, Daniel took in long, slow breaths. She put a hand on his shoulder, then pulled away as if burned. An inner debate began in her mind. She was supposed to be helping win this man over to her grandfather's plan, not making things worse by making him sick. She couldn't imagine anything worse than puking your guts out. The new question, of course, was would having her here to watch only make things worse? Would her presence comfort him, or embarrass him? She wanted to do the right thing, but she didn't have a clue.

The door slid open and Craig came out onto the deck holding out his hand. "Motion sickness medicine. Should help, at least take the edge off."

Daniel's best effort at a smile looked more like a grimace. "Thanks." He accepted the chewable pill and popped it in his mouth. She'd feel a lot better about this if his knuckles weren't still white on the railing.

"I should have asked if you wanted to sail. We all grew up spending as much time on water as on dry land. We love it, some more than others. I swear Siobhan was a fish in her previous life. Still, it simply never occurred to any of us to check with you first."

He must have felt a little better because he chuckled. "Sounds like my family on ice."

"Everyone skates in your family?" She knew his brother was a pro hockey player but she hadn't read much about the rest of his family.

He nodded briskly and the way he slammed his eyes shut, she knew he'd instantly regretted it. Sucking in a long slow breath, he blew it out equally slowly. "We're Canadians. Skating is in our DNA."

That made her chuckle. A part of her knew he was only kidding, and yet another part of her believed his every word. "Even your mom?"

A sly grin pulling at one side of his mouth, he barely dipped his chin in a single affirmative motion. "She was one heck of a goalie. Taught me everything I know." His gazed wandered off to an unknown point in the distance. "When conditions weren't right to skate outdoors, my dad would flood the basement, let it freeze, and send my brother and me downstairs to practice."

"I know this sounds silly, but of all the mothers in this family, the one I can see doing that is Grams."

"Really?"

She nodded. "The words 'tough old broad' come to mind. In the nicest way possible, of course."

He chuckled. "Of course."

"It takes a lot to be married to a Marine and raise six children on your own. She was up to the task as a parent and with all the drama in her adult children's lives, she was a rock for us grandchildren." Her cheeks tugged at her lips. "And she really knows her poker."

That made Daniel cackle out loud. "The well-dressed, polite, and dare I say delicate woman I met earlier today does not line up with the vision of cigar smoke filled room and the sound of chips clanking or the smell of beer and whisky."

"Don't let her fool you. She can drink any Marine under the table if necessary, and she remembers cards as easily as her descendant's birthdays."

"It's sweet how much you love her."

Her head tipped sideways. "Don't you love your grandmother?"

"Very much. She's the walking example of unconditional love."

"Then why does it surprise you that I love my grandmother so much?"

His gaze dropped and his shoulders hefted up in a lazy shrug. "I guess I allowed myself to fall into the mindset of the typical rich stereotype."

"And what is that?"

"Well, for new money there's the assumption that every athlete is dumb and going to blow his income on fancy cars, big houses, and be broke in no time at all. With old money families, like the Barons, the assumption is that money matters more than family, power matters more than money, and the peasants should eat cake if they can't afford bread."

She couldn't help the grimace that stretched across her face or the sharp intake of breath that accompanied it. "Ooh."

"Yeah." He slowly shook his head. "I've learned a lot in a couple of days with your family. Mostly I've learned there's much to be said for the old cliché 'don't judge a book by its cover'."

"Fair enough." It wasn't news to her that many people assumed the ultra wealthy were spoiled brats with deep pockets. But she had to admit it hurt more this time to hear it from Daniel. Which, considering she'd known him less than two days, her gut reaction made no sense.

"I probably shouldn't have said anything at all. As a matter of fact, normally I would have kept my opinions to myself, but for whatever reason, the words just came out. Would it help any if I said I'm sorry?" The look in his eyes seemed to hold as much hurt as she felt.

Somehow, seeing the sincerity in his words, the unexpected hurt did indeed lift. "Apology accepted."

"Tell me more about your adventures at sea." He smiled at her.

"No. I think we need to get the captain to turn the Baroness around and get you back on dry land."

He shook his head. This time, no grimace or second thoughts. "No. Whatever your brother gave me seems to have done the trick. We can't change things up now. The committee and the Governor have gone to a great deal of trouble to show me what a wonderful place the Houston area is."

"Is it working?" She couldn't help the cheesy smile that erupted.

His grin widened, he turned away from the railing, and settling his hand on the small of her back, redirected her toward the cabin door. "I'll let you know when I know."

Thinking of his day on the boat brought a smile to Daniel's face. Considering his brother had teased him most of his life over his propensity to get seasick, he knew Henry would be laughing his rear off at Daniel's shock to discover the day in Galveston had meant a day on the family yacht. Having spent so much of their lives at each other's hips, it wasn't a surprise that just thinking about Henry had Daniel's phone ringing and Henry on the other end. "Hey, bro."

Thankfully, whatever pill Craig had given him had conquered his seasickness so he could thoroughly enjoy the day in the Gulf. Spending time on the yacht was far from a hardship, as long as he wasn't hanging over the railing spilling his guts.

"Hey, big bro. I keep waiting to hear an update. We're all wondering where we're moving to. You're in Houston now, right?

"I am."

"How's it going?"

That all depended on what 'it' was. The city, the Barons, the team, or the woman who was very quickly working her way under his skin and he had no idea why. "Houston itself is good."

"Hmm. I detect a deflection? What's going on?"

Daniel sank further into the oversized chair in the living area. The Houston committee, or more likely the Barons, had seen fit to set him up in not only one of the best hotels Houston had to offer. As for the chair, it was so darn comfortable he actually wondered if he could buy one just like it. "So far, Houston is going over the top to win me over."

"Hmm. I guess you're entitled to some perks for hauling your butt all over the country for this team. How over the top?"

"Let's say I'm getting an unexpected view of what Houston has to offer thanks to the Barons."

"Barons? There's royalty in Houston?"

"I'm starting to think so. Except Baron is the family name and they really, really want the Comets here."

"Doesn't everyone?"

"Maybe, but so far no one seems to have the backing that Houston has." He wouldn't be surprised if along with a ready-to-go stadium, and appealing tax breaks, the Barons didn't offer something ridiculous like paying team salaries for the first few years. If he'd learned one thing in the last two days it was that the Barons could probably afford to buy their own country, never mind a hockey team.

"If anyone can put up with a committee of cigar smoking old farts trying to win the team over, you can do it."

The thought of Page smoking a cigar made him smile. Not exactly an old fart by anyone's standards. Though technically she wasn't part of the committee, it was clear if her family wanted a hockey team in Houston, then so did she. Still, hockey or no hockey, he was pretty sure she was as intrigued by him as he was with her. So much so, that instead of flying home for a few days before his next stop, he was thinking of just staying in Houston. How crazy was that? "If you mean that I paid my dues by getting slammed into the boards and bringing my team to the Stanley Cup more than once qualifies me for battling with committee members, yeah, I guess so."

"How hard are they trying?"

"They've put me up in a suite in a five-star hotel."

"Nothing unusual about that."

"I don't mean a junior suite. I'm talking Prince William, his family, and staff kind of suite."

Henry whistled. "How do I get your job?"

How Daniel got booted out of hockey was not something he would ever wish on his kid brother—luxury suite or no luxury suite. Without thinking, he reached down to rub his knee. Funny, it hadn't bothered him much at all since arriving in Houston. Probably all that heat he thought he would hate. "You don't want it."

"A few days of high living is something I could get used to."

His brother didn't know the half of it. "Should I mention they took me out on their yacht yesterday?"

"Yacht?"

"Yep. Moored in the Gulf of Mexico."

Henry started to cackle with laughter. "I'm sorry. You on a boat?"

"It's a ship. Boats are smaller."

"Potato patahtoh. You get seasick in a bathtub."

"Okay, no need to exaggerate."

"Who's exaggerating?" The words came through with more laughter.

"They gave me some pill. Worked like a charm. They took me for a spin around the gulf. It was nice."

"Nice? Just nice? How big a yacht?"

They'd told him, but somewhere between wanting to puke his guts out and awed at the degree of luxury, he'd forgotten. "Let's say Greek tycoons have nothing on Texas Barons."

Henry whistled again. "So is the team moving to Houston?"

His brother was teasing; Henry knew there was more to his job than who could schmooze better than the others. Or who had the granddaughter with the most captivating smile and cutting sense of humor.

"Okay. What's taking so long to answer? That was a joke, but now I'm not so sure. What aren't you telling me?"

"There's a lot to consider. They have a stadium ready to go. They're willing to build bigger and better with tax payer and private money. There's no shortage of hotels for fan and team accommodations. Houston has a major airport hub. The idea of a rivalry between Dallas and Houston does hold appeal."

"But…"

And that's where his brother knew him too well. Daniel rubbed a hand down his face. He shared a lot with his brother. Almost everything. But he wasn't ready to share Paige yet. And he wasn't ready to admit that the lines between what was best for the team and what was bet for him were starting to blur. The question was, what was he going to do about that?

CHAPTER SEVEN

Nothing about Paige's day had gone as planned. Despite having climbed into bed at a decent hour, she hadn't gotten anything close to a good night's sleep. Instead she'd tossed and turned, and had strange dreams about dancing in fields of bluebonnets with one especially good-looking former hockey player. Who the heck danced in bluebonnets anyway?

On today's agenda, the Governor had given her the day off to actually do her job. Since she had zero interest in touring the hotel options in and around the arena, she was happy to be able to get back to the thing she loved—making great wine. Of course the catch was that for the better part of her day, she'd been frequently distracted with thoughts of Daniel. For a man who once made his living in what she'd considered a Neanderthal sport, he had proven to be charming, smart, funny, and... well, sweet. And was very quickly worming his way into her world.

Finally she decided the only thing to keep her mind off Daniel and on her job and the upcoming competition would be to venture down to the cellar and play with her new wines. Despite the miserable clay soil in Texas, she'd spent a small fortune to build a good old fashioned wine cellar just below the tank room so the wine could age in it, as well as properly store some of her best blends.

Shaking her thoughts of former hockey stars out of her mind, Paige straightened and actually said a silent little prayer. She'd just poured the liquid from a tank and hoped some characteristic of the grape that she'd liked before pressing would still be in the flavor after fermentation. Swirling the glass in her hand, she stared at the contents.

The fine coating of sugar on the inside of the glass did not have quite the consistency she had strived for. The color was good but the legs on it weren't exactly where she wanted them to be, but that was a lesser concern. She stuck her nose into the glass and took a large breath. If she liked the taste now, a barrel would be next for this vintage.

Her prized cellar had two doors, one upstairs, discretely blended into the paneled wall, and another downstairs at the entrance to where she'd been playing with her wines. About to take notes on her observations, the rattling sound of the door handle across the large room caught her attention, followed by a soft thud and then a few quick bangs. Someone was taking great efforts to open it. Setting down the glass, she trudged over. Giving the door a strong tug, one of Paige's employees burst into the room. Running her hand along the side of the door, she turned to face her boss. "How long has that been sticking?"

Paige sighed. "A while. Probably the humidity. It never ends in Houston."

"I'll make a note to have maintenance deal with this."

Paige should probably have done that herself, but somehow, compared to everything else going on at the winery, the door had never held much importance. "No need. I'll handle it."

Her employee nodded.

"Did you need something?"

"No. I was just checking on you before I leave. I'd stay till you're done, but the wind has picked up. It's probably nothing, but I'm heading home."

"Thanks. Lock up the tasting room, I'll take care of everything else."

"Don't work too late." Her employee waited for Paige to nod in agreement before turning toward the door. She probably knew as well as Paige did that some days when she was engrossed in a project, staying until all hours of the night was nothing unusual. "I'll prop the door open."

"Thanks." Her mind already back on the vintage she was working on, she tossed a, "thank you" over her shoulder, returning to the table where the glass sat. Pulling a stool closer, she examined the wine under the light and sighed. The color was ruby red. She'd hoped the Cabernet grape she'd used would have been darker.

Frowning at the glass, she said one more prayer and hoped that perhaps the taste would be better than the color implied. She took a sip and as she held the liquid in her mouth, the wine coated her tongue. The flavor was smooth and fruity, and when she swallowed, the finish delighted her.

Now hunched over the table, she scribbled tasting notes on an index card. Once again, the rattling of the door knob disturbed her peace. Now what? Intent on her notes, she dismissed the sounds.

The rattling grew in intensity and she remembered all the employees had gone for the day. Her pen stilled over the card. She blinked, dragging her mind away from wine and focused on her dark and isolated surroundings. This time the rattling had been replaced by the scraping of something heavy against the concrete floor. It had never occurred to her to put a panic button in this room. Or at least an intercom. Of course that wouldn't do her any good if there was no one else in the building.

Looking up toward the darkened stairwell, a light tapping that had replaced the rattles and scrapes, gave way to a stronger knocking and someone clearing their throat. Surely bad guys didn't clear their throats? Actually, bad guys wouldn't have made near so much noise. Just in case, she pushed to her feet and reached for a nearby bottle of wine. Noticing the blend, she shook her head and setting it down, grabbed an inferior bottle she'd never liked, and held it up in the air. "Who's there?"

"Me, Daniel."

Rolling her eyes, she set the bottle down before anyone noticed she'd been watching too many horror flicks with women too stupid to live hiding out in dark basements. In a few short steps, she came within view of the door. Sure enough, Daniel stood there, a grin on his face, and a bag of something in his hands.

"My designated committee member and guide for today

had to call it an early day. His son dislocated a shoulder during football practice. I called ahead and a friendly young woman said she was on her way out the door but I'd probably find you working down here. Clay let me in." He held up a bag in each hand. "I brought some dinner."

Her mouth watered and her stomach grumbled. "I guess I may have forgotten to eat today. Come on in." She turned back toward the table and waved him in, remembering the sticking door a fraction after she heard the latch catch.

Daniel took in the expression on her face, followed her gaze to the door, and faced her again. "Is something wrong?"

"Let's hope not." Strolling past him, she reached for the handle and gave the door a good tug. Nothing. Trying again, still nothing.

"Let me." Daniel repeated her efforts and the door wasn't anymore cooperative than it had been with her. Slowly turning on his heels, he leveled his gaze with hers. "To quote Tom Hanks, 'Houston, we have a problem.'"

There were two ways to look at the stuck door. Yes, being unable to open the door was a problem. On the other hand, it was also an opportunity to spend alone time with Paige. Very alone. Not that he would have done anything like this on purpose, but if fate saw fit to lock out the real world, who was he to argue?

"This is so not good. I really should have put in a panic button." She was trying to make light of the problem, but he could hear the concern in her voice.

"I suppose it's a moot point now, but I for one don't problem solve well on an empty stomach."

Her gaze spun around to meet his. "What?"

"I have dinner." He gestured toward where he'd set the two bags down. "We'll both think better after we've eaten, then we can brainstorm our way out of here.

Paige's shoulders dropped and he knew he'd sold her on

eating now, escaping later. Slowly, her chin dipped in reluctant agreement. "Okay. We'll eat. I'm not sure I can think straight anyway." She glanced once more at the door before following him to the table where a lamp lit up the surface along with a few bottles and a glass.

"Do you always work late?" The way everyone had spoken about her this evening, he was pretty certain he already knew the answer.

She slid a stool over to the table for him and then settled on her own. "I'm trying this vintage. I'm figuring out if it's ready for barrel aging or not."

Reaching for the bags of food on the table, Daniel began to unpack their dinner. "I didn't know what you liked so I got a little bit of everything." With all the food spread out on the small table, he looked up from the silence and into Paige's wide eyes.

"Did you buy out the whole store?"

Her honest surprise made him laugh. "Close to it. For a major grocery store, Central Market is pretty cool."

"And popular."

"I can see why. I must admit, I didn't expect anything like that in Houston."

"Why not? You do realize we are the fourth largest city in the United States."

He pulled out paper plates and silverware from another bag. "I know but, what can I say, the selection surprised me."

Glancing down at the spread of food continuing to come out of the bags like objects out of Mary Poppins' suitcase, her jaw momentarily fell open. "Good grief, you really did buy everything."

"I wanted to make sure I brought options you'd like." It had been a stress point for him standing in the supermarket. He'd never wanted to charm a woman as much as he wanted to charm Paige. Somewhere between the last hotel and the market, he'd decided without any doubt that he was not going home between visiting cities, and hockey had nothing to do with the decision. That realization was almost as scary as the decision itself.

As he opened the containers of pesto salad, antipasto, and other warm and cold foods that covered the gamut from vegetarian to carnivore, Paige held out a bottle of wine. "Shall I open this?"

He shrugged. "You're the expert. If you pick it, I'm sure it will be delicious."

"I'll get the glasses." Her lips tipped up at the corners and his chest puffed with satisfaction at the delight dancing in her eyes.

Leaning over the small table, almost close enough to kiss the dab of pesto from the corner of her lips, he shoved an olive in his mouth before he did something stupid and scared her off for good. Swallowing, he took a sip from his glass. "Wow, this is delicious."

"Thank you." Her smile spread.

"How did you get into the wine business? I mean, I assume the family, but…"

"It was sort of by accident. My grandfather had been buying wine from here for decades. Then, in recent years he noticed things were deteriorating. The wine was still delicious, but with cracks in the walls and leaks in the roof, shoppers weren't as loyal."

"I can understand that." He reached for a roasted pepper.

"Anyhow, one day the Governor offered to help the owners out and rather than accept his help, they offered to sell it to him, lock stock and wine barrels. And he did."

"And that's how you became a vintner?"

"Not exactly." She shrugged, an olive pit slipped from between her lips, and he almost swallowed his tongue. "He'd thought my younger cousin Trevor, one of my Uncle Oliver's six kids, would be well suited. He was just finishing up his MBA and entertaining different options."

"But?"

"He didn't know the difference between Pinot Noir and Pinot Grigio and didn't care to learn."

"Okay, even I know one is red and one is white."

Her smile bloomed again. "That's right. Very good."

"I thought everyone knew that."

She shook her head. "Anyhow, Grams mentioned to my grandfather that I'd visited a lot of wineries on a tour of France and that perhaps he should consider a granddaughter instead of a grandson."

"And the rest is history?"

"Pretty much. That was six years ago and I've never looked back." She picked up another olive. "What about you? You don't play hockey anymore?" It wasn't really a question.

"No. The car accident did quite a number on my leg. It's a miracle I don't walk with a limp or anything." He could still take a simple turn around the rink, but that was all.

"You miss it." Again, the question wasn't a question at all.

"Just every day. Very little can compare with the feeling of sailing on ice, reaching the puck, finding all the players aligned, and one good swing sends the puck flying over the goalie's outstretched hand and into the belly of the net. Win or lose, the adrenaline high after a game lasts for hours. There's no going home and collapsing into bed. Every sense is alive and on fire. It takes time to get over that loss, and in my case, not playing with my brother anymore. Those were special years." He didn't like letting himself wander down memory lane. Thinking about what could have been. It took him a long while to appreciate what he'd had and not resent what he'd missed. "There are some positives to leaving the ice for a desk job."

"And what would that be?" He loved the sincere interest sparkling in her eyes.

"For one thing," he actually found himself smiling. It was nice to feel at peace with where he was in his life now. "No one slams me into the boards anymore so I don't need to bathe in ice. I'll probably get to keep all my teeth into my old age, and my laundry room doesn't smell like a locker room." He almost laughed out loud at the last point. He'd actually kept an entire room in his house to air out his equipment between games. "Truth is, I'm truly blessed to still be in the business of hockey."

"But?"

"No buts."

One brow rose higher than the other, but she didn't say a word, just waited for him to say something.

Hefting a shoulder in a lazy shrug, he had no idea if she could read his mind or his heart, but he started to wonder. "I guess the whole truth is that yes, I love my job, I'm extremely thankful to still be in professional hockey, but I've kicked around whether or not switching to coaching would be a good move for me."

"What's stopping you?"

Wasn't that a great question. "I don't know if being that close to the ice, the action, would be good for my soul, or if not being able to actually play would only make me miss the game even more."

"I guess," she reached for her glass and stared up at him from over the rim, "there's only one way to find out."

The woman was right. He knew that. In five minutes she'd summed up what he'd been circumventing since he first stepped into the Comet's home office.

"So," she set the glass down and smiled at him. "How'd you wind up as point man on this? I would think going from city to city and having anxious committees douse you with promises teeters somewhere between exhausting and boring."

"Well, so far, Houston has been anything but."

Her eyes widened, her mouth dropped slightly open and suddenly lips never looked so kissable. His gaze leveled with hers and he swore he saw the same yearning in her eyes that was pushing him forward, prompting him to take a chance and kiss the woman.

Only an inch away from tasting heaven, a familiar scraping noise filled the room, followed by the loud banging of a heavy door against the wall. "There you are."

Both Daniel and Paige sprang apart like a pair of bouncing electrons. The man he remembered as the winery manager crossed the cavernous room. Not that Daniel wanted to remain trapped all night, but he couldn't help wishing that their rescuer had waited at least a little longer to set them free.

"Whose side are you on?" her brother Craig's voice boomed from the dashboard of her car.

"It's been a long day. What the heck are you talking about?"

"Hockey." Craig's voice went up an octave before he took in a deep, hopefully calming breath. "You're supposed to be helping convince Daniel that the Comets belong in Houston. Instead, you've tried to feed steak to a vegetarian, put the man who gets seasick on a yacht, and now you've locked him in a basement."

"Not a basement. The wine cellar. And to be perfectly clear, no one told me he was a vegetarian, or that he gets seasick, and we had a very nice dinner in the cellar."

"Who has a nice dinner in a dark cellar?"

"It wasn't dark." There was no way she was going to tell her brother that it was all about the company, not the place.

"Sis, this is super important to the Governor. And the city. And—"

"Yes. I know." She cut him off before he ran through a list of every politician in the state who was on board with this effort. "You don't need to remind me, but I'm not the one who made reservations or who scheduled a day on the yacht."

Craig's deep sigh carried through the phone line. "I'm sorry. But did you have to lock him in the cellar?"

"Do you want to take over?"

"I don't have the legs for the job." A bit of humor seeped into her brother's words. "What I do think is from now on, we need to double check the itinerary."

"Tomorrow is the ranch."

"Right. Okay. That shouldn't be a problem. I'm sure by now the Governor has corrected the vegetarian issue, but please, try not to let anything else happen to him."

Like she had any control over the man or his job. "Will do."

"And sis…"

"Yes?"

"Love you."

Why did her brothers always have to make her smile when she wanted to stay angry at them for at least a little bit? "Love you too."

CHAPTER EIGHT

Once they'd been freed by the winery manager, dinner had been cut short. Some problem or other with the weather forecast had the man pulling Paige away to deal with an issue. Kissable lips pressed tight, Paige barely shook her head and waved at the food. "Thanks for the thought, but this may take awhile. You might as well take it home and I'll see you tomorrow?"

"At the ranch." Daniel nodded, seriously wishing the guy had waited a little longer to uncover the problem of the hour. "That's the plan."

Her gaze darted from the food on the table to her manager waiting patiently at the door and back to him. "I really am sorry."

Again, he bobbed his head. "No problem. But don't forget to eat."

She'd done her best to offer what he hoped was a grateful smile and then turned away. Single file, they'd marched up the stairs and out the door. He'd given her one final wave before driving off to his very lonely hotel.

The morning light had him awake and dressed long before his alarm went off. The scheduled agenda for today had Daniel standing in front of the ranch home that reminded him more of a Southern antebellum house than home on the range, he hoped arriving a few minutes early wasn't a problem. He also hoped they didn't mistake his eagerness to see Paige again with his opinions on Houston's chances with the team.

A young woman he remembered to be one of Paige's sisters opened the door. "I hear you had a bit of an adventure last night. Glad to see you survived."

He chuckled. "I survived."

"Clay took the door off its hinges so it won't lock anyone else in." She pointed a thumb at her chest. "I'm Siobhan."

"Yes, I remember." No point mentioning he'd remembered the face not the name.

"I'm surprised. There's a whole pack of us. Keeping us straight is not an easy task."

From the foyer he followed her into a large, what someone might call family room, though the size seemed more suited to a hotel lobby.

"Hey," Paige called out from across the room, waving her arm toward a scattering of people. "You remember everyone. For those who haven't met our guest yet, this is Daniel."

Various hellos, and a howdy or two, were shouted in his direction.

He gave a quick wave and settled on a simple response of, "Hi."

On her feet, Paige waved him over. "We'll be mostly outside today."

Following her onto the rear patio, he was just as impressed today as he'd been the first time he'd seen the yard. The sun shone brightly and as many people as had been inside, were spread around outside. Glancing up at the cloudless blue sky, he shook his head. "I thought the forecast was for rain all week."

Paige laughed and shook her head. "It wouldn't dare rain on the Governor's outdoor plans. After all, he always—"

"Gets what he wants." They both laughed at what had now become an inside joke, but he was starting to see there was more to that little phrase than mere semantics. The smell of grilled meats drifted over to him. His first time in the yard he hadn't noticed the outdoor kitchen to the far end of the patio.

"We Texans love our beef." Paige had followed the direction of his gaze. "The Governor has been smoking pork for hours." Grinning, she spun to face him. "He's also got a stack of veggie burgers and some plant based something or other. I think you'll be pleased."

He chuckled. Rich, powerful, thoughtful, and the man smoked his own meats instead of catering. This family was truly an anomaly to what Daniel knew of the rich and famous.

Today, the backyard also sported the addition of a volleyball net. Not far away a horseshoe pit had been set up. A familiar face, her brother Craig waved at him before he took a shot at getting a ringer.

"I gather we're playing volleyball?"

A huge smile on her face, her head bobbed up and down. "Next game starts in a couple of minutes."

"Who's playing?" People he assumed were more family had begun to position themselves on the sand-covered squares.

A sweet chuckle tickled his eardrums. "We are. It's the over thirties verses the under thirties. We're counting on you to be in better shape than the rest of us overs."

"So, I'm supposed to be the ringer?"

Her chuckle bloomed into a full fledged laugh. "Smart man."

The overs and unders were already lined up on the court, ready for battle. Daniel picked up the volleyball and tossed it lightly in the air a few times getting a feel for it. He hadn't played in over a decade—hopefully, like riding a bicycle, it wouldn't matter. On a deep breath, he served the ball. Their point.

"You're good at this." Paige smiled over at him.

He smiled. "I might know a thing or two." He served again and this time the other team hit the ball back.

"Paige set."

Using her fingertips, Paige hit the ball straight into the air. Daniel jumped, spiking the ball just past Siobhan. The feisty redhead pointed with two fingers to her eyes and then turned them to point back at him.

This was proving to be more fun than he'd expected when he'd been invited to a family barbecue. Daniel served again and Paige let out a loud whoop. This time Siobhan spiked it past Paige. They lost the serve.

Holding the ball in her hand and glancing over the net and back, Siobhan served the ball right to Daniel, gleefully shouting, "In your face!"

Daniel laughed so hard he almost missed digging back over the net.

"Take that!" Paige shouted to her kid sister.

A friendly war of words went back and forth as often as the ball. Despite the competitive streak that ran strong in the Baron gene pool, this was a family who clearly loved each other. Having more money than Croesus hadn't made the Barons much different than the Duprees. He'd only grown up with one sibling, and even though the four of them were pretty tight when it came to hockey, he couldn't help but think, if he'd grown up with a passel of siblings, his family most likely would have been very much like this. Who'd have guessed, such very different families and lifestyles, and yet, not that different at all.

The day had been one heated game after another. If Daniel hadn't once upon a time been a professional hockey player, she doubted he would have been able to not only keep up, but manage to show off a time or two. So far he'd risen to every challenge presented to him. Next was cornhole.

Paige smiled up at him. "Have you played *this* before?"

"I'm familiar with it." Daniel smiled. "But my youth was spent mostly with a stick in my hand. I wouldn't go placing any wagers on my pitching skills."

"Would you have said the same about volleyball?" Her eyes flashed with humor.

All he said was, "Touché."

"All right then." She spun around and pointed to the boards set up several feet away. "One point for a bag on the board. Three points if the bag goes in the hole."

Daniel hefted the bean bag in his hand. "Got it."

"I'll be on your team."

Siobhan shook her head. "No way. Paige is a champ. I

call girls against boys."

"How fair would that be?" As much as she would love to trounce the men, a part of her wanted to spend as much time with Daniel as possible. She didn't analyze it. She didn't over think it. She simply wanted to go for it. "This way everything will balance out in the end."

Siobhan frowned. "I don't know. I smell a ringer."

Set up at her side, Daniel studied the distance to the boards and the weight of the bags as if he were calculating sending a rocket to the moon. His brows knit together and his eyes narrowed. It was the most serious Paige had ever seen him.

"Any year now!" Siobhan called from the other board.

His gaze swung to her, and he flashed a sizzling smile. "I can't let my teammate down."

The words echoed around her. Her heart did a double kick. There was no doubt from the look in his eyes that he was talking about more than a game. The way a Marine never left a man behind—ever—under any circumstance, she knew as sure as her name was Paige Baron, that Daniel Dupree wouldn't let anyone down. He wouldn't let her down. She almost couldn't catch her breath. Had anyone outside of her family ever made her feel so secure?

"All right, then," Siobhan shouted. "Let's see what he's got."

Daniel squared his shoulder and threw the first bag. It landed on the inside edge of the hole.

Siobhan narrowed her gaze and muttered, "I think we've been hustled."

The boyish grin Daniel flashed Paige tickled her to her core. He was proud of his throw. "Go again."

With concentration written on his face, he threw the second bag. It landed near the first one. This time he didn't smile, just nodded as if to say that was where he'd been aiming.

"Ha," Siobhan scoffed from across the way. "You're in Texas now, eh. Don't mess with Texas."

"We'll see about how tough Texas is." Daniel tossed the next two bags and each landed a hole in one.

High fives flew, along with comments about 'Canucks' and 'All Hats No Cattle.' Her siblings and Daniel had her almost doubled over in laughter.

Shaking her head at Daniel and flashing that smile, Siobhan crossed her arms. "How are you at 'Smores?"

"Smores?" Daniel turned to Paige. "Is this a competition too?"

Slightly bent over, catching her breath from laughing, her arms still around her waist, Paige moved her hands to her knees and glanced up at Daniel with one eye. "Probably."

"Is everything always a competition with you guys?"

"You're just figuring that out?" Paige straightened, brushed her hands together to wipe off the chalk from tossing the bean bags, and smiled at Daniel. "That's why in the end, Barons always get what they want."

Siobhan and her brother walked away to where the Governor in an oversized chef's hat and white apron that covered him from chin to cowboy boots was doling out lunch.

Daniel's gaze drifted to their departing backs and back to Paige. Slowly, that lazy smile that could make any woman weak in the knees teased at the corners of his mouth. "And what do you want, Paige?"

Her mouth suddenly went dry and her palms began to sweat. Wasn't that a loaded question?

"Was the question that hard?"

Was it?

"Tell you what." He set the beanbags on a table beside the cornhole boards. "Let me show you a piece of my world."

That question was easy. She shook her head. "I don't have time to go to Canada."

A deep rumble of laughter made his eyes sparkle. "I was thinking of something a little closer. Do you own a pair of skates?"

"Skates?" Intuition, or maybe plain common sense, told her she was going to like where this conversation was going.

"Never mind. I'll pick you up at ten tomorrow morning. Wear a warm jacket."

"But today is the last day scheduled for your Houston visit. I thought tomorrow you had to leave for the next city?"

He shrugged. "Don't have to be anywhere for several days. This is as good a place as any to do laundry."

There was absolutely no reason for such a ridiculous statement to make her heart leap and her cheeks tug hard at the corners of her mouth, but they did. He wanted to stay longer, and she sure as hell hoped it had to do with her and not hockey.

CHAPTER NINE

Today would have been the beginning of his between-city break. Time to do laundry, check the snail mail, and maybe consider what he'd seen so far. His brain needed time to recharge before the next run of cities with overeager committee members anxious to bring the team to their hometown. Though he seriously doubted any city could compete with the welcome Houston had shown him. And he knew for darn sure there wasn't another woman like Paige anywhere else in the country.

Who was he kidding; Paige was one of a kind anywhere in the world. He'd known plenty of women in his lifetime, some more interesting or beautiful than others, but none who made every nerve ending in his body feel so alive, who made his mind stop and think twice before opening his mouth and letting any stupidity tumble out, who doled out surprises as easily as a mother doled out love.

Which meant, rather than going home to an empty house, here he was spending another day with Paige. From the moment he'd picked up a razor and stared at his ugly mug in the mirror, to the second he'd pulled up in front of Paige's condo, a contented smile had remained firmly in place.

"You look like the cat that swallowed the canary." She returned the smile as he opened the car door for her.

Circling the hood, he dashed between raindrops and climbed into the driver side, and still grinning, turned to her. "No canary. Just know it's going to be a good day."

"Oh? I sure hope you know what you're talking about."

Pulling out onto the main road, he slapped an open-faced hand onto his chest. "Uh, she doubts we'll have a good day together."

"No!" Her voice jumped an octave. "That's not what I meant at all. It's just that, I mean…" She sighed. "The only thing you mentioned was skates."

He felt the pull of his cheeks against his lips once again. "That would be because we're going ice skating."

The sound of air whistling between her lips as she winced was almost enough to make him change his mind. Almost.

"Just so there's no surprise, I don't know how to ice skate."

"First of all, I thought Houston is supposed to be a filled with ice hockey fans. Folks who love everything ice-skating."

The way all color drained suddenly from her face almost made him laugh.

"That's different." She squirmed, tugging at the safety belt across her shoulder. "I've never been very sports minded."

"Could have fooled me." A sports gene seemed to dominate the Baron gene pool. He reached over and gently tapped the top of her hand, wishing he could keep her hand in his. "Relax. I'm only teasing. Even in the Northeast, there are plenty of people who don't skate. Have you ever been rollerblading?"

"As a kid, yeah. But let's say I left that pastime behind with my braces."

"You wore braces?" Somehow he'd just assumed every Baron was born perfect, right down to their teeth.

"Doesn't everyone?"

"I suppose." He had never considered braces much and had no intention of doing so now. "If you were any good at rollerblading, skating on ice won't be much harder once you get the hang of it."

"If you say so." She didn't look terribly convinced.

The rink wasn't far from Paige's home. Choosing a parking spot under one of the few shade trees in the concrete lot, he hurried to open the car door and then forced himself not to reach for her hand as they walked into the building.

"Ooh." She hugged herself, rubbing her arms. "This is colder than I expected."

"You'll warm up once we're moving on the ice."

She shot him a sideways glance that told him she wasn't holding out much hope that he was right. Or maybe she wasn't expecting to spend that much time on the ice.

Since everyone working the rink seemed to know who he was, the man in charge of the skate rentals actually moved to the back of the shop and personally sharpened the skates he and Paige would be wearing.

Another few minutes and he helped her with her skates, lacing them up nice and tight. "This will support your ankles better, make it easier to maneuver."

"Maneuver?" She made a sound that might have been a chuckle. "I'll be lucky if I can stand."

"Now, now." He slapped the side of her booted ankle, set her foot on the ground, and pushed to his feet. "Here we go."

Even though walking on the rubber matted floors wasn't too difficult, she wobbled enough to warrant an offer to hold her hand. When she eagerly snatched hold of his hand, he decided this had been his best idea yet.

At the entry to the ice, she stopped in her tracks. "I don't know about this."

"It'll be fine. You'll see."

Heaving a deep sigh, he could see her strapping on the Baron determination he'd been used to seeing. Pulling away from his hand, she grabbed onto the side and put one foot on the ice.

Before he could suggest she wait for him to hold her hand again, that one leg shot forward, the other flew sideways, and arms flailing, she dropped onto the ice like a landed trout. Panic coursed through his veins. Maybe this wasn't his best idea?

"Easy, huh?" Due to years of being tackled by older

brothers in flag football—where tackling wasn't allowed— she managed to land, if not gracefully, at least without breaking a bone.

"Are you okay?" The sheer panic in his voice almost had her bursting with laughter.

Only the thick blanket of embarrassment kept her teeth gritted instead. "I'm fine." But smart enough to know if she moved at all she'd only take another face plant. "I could use some help up, though."

His hands had already gripped her arms and now he yanked her up with the same ease she might have lifted a feather. "I really am sorry. It will be better if you let me hold your hand."

"You want me to do this again?" Even she could hear the horror in her own voice.

"Well," he had the good graces to suppress a smile, "maybe not exactly that."

She couldn't help it. After years of being the younger sister, she did what came naturally and waved her arm, smacking him hard across the chest. "I'm not even going to apologize for that."

"Sorry. I'm the one who should be apologizing. Can I please try again?" He extended his hand. "Allow me to help. It will only take a few minutes to get the hang of it."

A small harrumph was the best she could manage. But she was a Baron, she could do this. That or her brothers would never let her hear the end of it. Hanging on to his hand with the same grip she might have used to hold onto the ledge of a building ten stories in the air, she dared follow him onto the ice.

For a fraction of a second, one foot threatened to wobble out from under her as her torso made a frantic effort to keep herself balanced, when she felt his weight glide around her. Before she knew what had happened, he stood on the opposite side. The hand holding her now rested on her back, while his other hand tightly gripped hers, allowing him to hold her straight and upright. Even more surprising, they were very slowly gliding forward.

"See, not so hard," he spoke softly.

Not completely convinced she wasn't going to fall, they'd made it halfway around the large rink before she felt herself relax just a little.

"Not so bad, is it?" The smooth gentleness, that a man might use with his frightened child, surprised her.

"I'll admit this is better than falling."

Though she didn't think her reply had been very positive, it brought a wide smile to his face nonetheless. *Men.* Would she ever understand them?

They'd made it completely around the rink twice when in that same gentle voice, he asked, "What do you say I move to your other side and we go around with me only holding your hands?" Panic must have risen in her eyes again because he quickly rambled, "Or we can keep doing this?"

If there was ever a time to put on her big girl panties, this was it. Taking in a deep breath and slowly exhaling, she shook her head. "No, it's okay. Let's try one hand."

Slowly, he maneuvered around her and gliding his right hand across her back as his left slid away, he quickly snatched her free hand in his right. How he made it all look so simple, she'd never understand. Then again, he'd once made his living on ice. She shouldn't be surprised if, like Cary Grant in the fifties holiday film, he suddenly skated away doing jumps and twirls.

"You're doing great."

Those words brought a smile to her face. She was doing better than she'd expected after her less than stellar first attempt on ice. "Thanks."

"No thanks necessary. You're doing all the hard work."

Not that she'd expected him to be a mean oaf or anything, but she hadn't expected such tenderness from him either. "Have you ever taught skating before?"

"Yes. One of my youth hockey coaches thought it was important character building skill for us to mentor younger players. I ended up with a kid who only skated because his dad wanted him to. Poor kid had no natural skill at all."

"That must have been hard?"

"For someone who could skate as easily as I breathed?

Yeah, but it also taught me a great deal about patience and appreciation for the skill I had."

"Sounds like the coach was right."

Daniel nodded, and for a moment seemed lost in another place and time. "After the required teaching time was over, Tommy asked me if I could help him without letting his father know. The kid wanted so badly to make his dad proud. Where Tommy was lacking in coordination, he made up for an entire team in the brains and personality department. He wasn't just a brilliant nerd, he was a social one. Had a great sense of humor for a ten year old."

"How old were you?"

Daniel shrugged. "Maybe fifteen."

"What did you say?"

His eyes widened round with surprise "Of course I said yes. It wasn't easy. Hockey practice and studies ate up most of my free time, but it made me mad as hell that his dad didn't appreciate what a great kid he had because he wasn't the hockey star the father had always wanted to be. I found the time."

Suddenly she was so appreciative of the love and support her whole family had given each other regardless of their strengths or weaknesses.

He blinked and a sweet smile crossed his lips. "Kid wound up teaching me that with a little determination and a lot of hard work, anything is possible." He turned to face her, his smile now wider than that on any of her family in a proud moment. "Tommy actually won MVP in the state tournament his senior year."

She should have known this man had a heart as big as the state of Texas. Bigger. That thought brought an odd flutter deep in the pit of her stomach that worked its way up her chest and was making itself at home in her heart. Boy, was she in trouble.

CHAPTER TEN

Leaning over, untying his laces, Daniel struggled with all the thoughts skating around in his head. Paige had proven to be a good sport, and for her first effort, not too bad a skater. He knew a lot of people who couldn't stand on ice to save their lives. He also doubted that she would want to make skating her next favorite hobby, but still he was proud of her efforts.

Her determination to skate not only reminded him of Tommy, in a very different way, it was one more thing that made Paige special. Very special. And he very much wanted to take her out again. Not on a business tour, not as new friend, but on a date. A real live, non business related, I really like you, date. And that for some reason was scaring the hell out of him.

Still leaning over his laces, he turned to see her slipping her foot out of her skate. "Do you have any plans tonight?"

Her skates in hand, she sat up and looked to him, shaking her head. "None."

Sucking in a bit of air and courage, he straightened in his seat and looked at her. "Would you join me for dinner tonight?" Blowing out a huff of annoyed air, he shook his head. "Let me rephrase that."

Her brows buckled, but she nodded.

Great. He was really mucking this up. "What I mean is, would you join me not for another business dinner, but for a date?" There, he'd said it.

Instantly, tense shoulders lowered and that sweet lazy smile that did weird things to his insides appeared. "I'd like that."

"Good." He pushed to his feet. "I found this place

online that looks like fun. The Kitchen Café."

"Oh, I've heard of it. Always gets good reviews, but I've never been. I think it used to be a favorite place of my brother Mitch and his wife."

"Really?" He had no idea if that was good or bad, but right now he was so happy she'd said yes that he didn't really care. "It said dinner served starting at seven and music starts at eight. Shall I pick you up at six?"

"Sounds perfect."

That's what he was shooting for. He hoped the place turned out to be as special as she was. In the meantime, he wondered if accepting a date meant he could now hold her hand. For a grown man, he was spending way too much time figuring out the simplest of things. A teen in high school would have less trouble figuring out what to do with a girl.

Of course, Paige was no girl, she was one hell of a woman. One he didn't want to lose. *Didn't want to lose.* He shook his head, decided now was not the time to hold her hand yet, and led the way to return the skates and take her home. Then he could go to his hotel and pace the floors until it was time to pick her up. Yep, a teenager would definitely be handling this better than he was.

It had only taken him an hour and half and changing three times before he decided he was being ridiculous. That's when he wound up at the men's store down the block. Like it or not, nothing that he had with him had been packed to impress a woman.

So here he sat in his car, hours later, with a woman he didn't want to lose, on the way to their very important first date, and he was tongue tied.

"I spoke with Mitch."

"Oh?"

"I'm usually hesitant to bring up anything about his late wife, it always seems to make him sad."

He didn't want to even think about how much pain losing his wife had cost the senator.

"He says we're going to love it. The owner is a wonderfully versatile musician who also loves to cook. We don't think he actually cooks anymore, but he plays every night and he and my sister-in-law loved it every time they went."

"Good, because here we are." A parking spot waited for them right in front. Since the rain hadn't let up all day, he hoped finding a premium space was a good sign for the night ahead of them.

"Oh, wow." Paige stepped into the club ahead of him and stopped. The lighting was just dark enough to fill a soul with a sense of calm, but not so dark to put a person to sleep. Tables for two and four were scattered about and could easily be pushed together for bigger groups. On each table a single fresh flower rested in a colorful vase.

All in all, he was hopeful. Especially when he read the one page menu. Three choices for appetizer, dinner, and dessert. All of them sounded both simple and delicious.

Paige ordered the glazed salmon and he opted for chipotle mac and cheese. After all, when in Texas.

"If that food is half as good as the description, we're going to be in for a treat." Paige placed the napkin across her lap. He had to agree.

For the next little while they chatted about everything from his first day at hockey camp when he met Wayne Gretzky and almost forgot how to skate, to her first barrel racing win—he should have known she was a champion in more ways than in his heart. From there they moved on to how he landed his current job with the Comets and Paige's excitement over an upcoming competition for the winery.

He cut into his mac and cheese at the same time Paige sliced into her salmon. One bite and he didn't know who had groaned louder with delight.

"Oh, wow. This is fantastic." Paige waved a fork at him.

"Mine too." He scooped up the next morsel with gusto. "So far so good."

"You're batting a thousand, Mr. Dupree."

That made him smile. He'd thought they were having a great time too, but hearing her say so made him want to do a jig.

"Oh," Paige perked up at the sound of a guitar note, "sounds like they're getting ready to start."

The first song was the "Girl from Ipanema." Not what he'd expected, but the way Paige swayed in her seat, he'd guess she was pleased. The next tune was one he recognized from Carole King sung by too many artists to remember, and when Paige began to sway in her seat once again, he reached across the table for her hand. "May I have this dance?"

Daniel's outstretched hand lingered in front of her for a moment before good sense kicked in and Paige took hold of it. A smile teased at his lips, and his eyes sparkled with delight. Not since her prom could she remember a date who willingly—or without extreme prodding—set foot on a dance floor.

She rose and returned the smile. "I'd like that."

His hand on her lower back, he guided her through the narrow path between tables. At the dance floor, the hand that had rested along her back, nudged her around and into the fold of his arms. His other hand folded around hers and resting her other hand on his shoulder, she marveled at how natural it felt to be standing with him like this.

Another couple made their way onto the floor. With unexpected ease, Daniel held her a fraction closer and maneuvered her around the growing number of dancers. She had to tell her feet to keep moving and resist the urge to nestle into his shoulder and simply enjoy the nearness of him. They were as intimate as they'd ever been, and yet, they were in a room full of strangers.

As the musicians picked up the beat for the chorus, Daniel took a step in retreat and twirled her in place, seamlessly bringing her back into his arms.

"Wow. Who knew Fred Astaire was alive and well and visiting Texas."

A slow chuckle rumbled in his chest. "I wouldn't go

quite that far, but in some ways, dancing isn't that different from ice hockey."

"I was just on an ice rink with you. Trust me when I say it's very different."

That made him chuckle a little harder. "It's all about balance, using your center of gravity, and yes, a sense of rhythm. The game has a rhythm to it."

"Rhythm? Hockey?" She tried her best not to laugh at the idea.

"Think about it. What do my fellow teammates do on skates? How do they move? They glide, almost sway. They're moving forward, one foot after the other, in synchronization like a metronome. You could almost imagine the players breaking into a dance routine."

"Okay," she shook her head, "I don't think we watch the same hockey games."

"Sure we do." He spun her about on the floor. "The puck just shot past me so I had to turn." Holding her a fraction closer they crossed the floor, one foot sliding in front of the other. "And now I have to beat out the next guy to reach the puck." Taking a step back, he twirled her the way he had when they first reached the floor. "Now the defensemen are trying to stop me from shooting at the goal, but with a little fancy footwork I'll shoot and score. Balance and rhythm dictate how I move. Keeps me on my feet."

"That might be the most creative analogy in reference to dancing I've ever heard."

"I'll take that as a compliment."

"It was." Each time they were together, she peeled back another layer of this complicated man. And each time, there was something more interesting underneath than the layer before. How could she ever grow tired of a man like this?

"Once," he continued, "I had a coach who suggested ballroom dancing to help improve our performance on the ice. I was the only one who tried it."

"Oh, your teammates must have had a field day with that."

His smile widened and his head bobbed up and down. "They kept hanging tiaras in my locker."

She couldn't stop from letting out a short laugh. She could imagine the entire scenario. What was that old adage; *what separates the men from the boys is the price of their toys.* "I'd bet you would look fetching with a tiara on."

Daniel groaned.

"Don't worry." She patted his shoulder. "Your secret is safe with me."

One song ended and seamlessly, another began. That was fine with her. Paige would have been delighted to stay this way forever.

As the music played, one couple passed by, the husband squinting at them. A moment later, that same couple spun around and craning his neck, the poor man practically fell over looking at them.

"I think you have a fan."

Without looking in the direction she pointed with her chin, Daniel shook his head. "No. He just can't get over how beautiful you are."

"Ha," she smiled, "does that line usually work for you?"

"Don't know. I don't ever say it."

The air grew suddenly thick around them. There wasn't a lick of humor in his eyes, only an intensity that seemed to see through to her soul.

"Excuse me." The man who had been twisting and turning to get a better view of Daniel finally stopped at their side. "You're Daniel Dupree?"

The way Daniel hesitated, for a moment she thought he was going to deny it, but he finally nodded. "I am."

"I thought so." The man let go of his wife and began fishing in his pockets. "Honey, do you have a pen and paper?"

Suddenly an arm appeared between them holding a napkin. At the other end, a much younger man stood smiling at them, making no pretense of wanting to dance. He couldn't have been more than twenty years old. "Could I have an autograph too, please?"

It hadn't taken long for murmurs to spread through the room and for Daniel to find himself back at the table signing napkins, coasters, and even the back of one man's shirt. When all those who wanted autographs had returned to their tables or to dancing, Daniel took a long sip of water and then, shaking his head, smiled at her. "I can't believe that just happened."

Paige held back a grin and shrugged. "We keep telling you this *is* a hockey town. Not can be." She leaned forward. "*Is.*"

For the life of her, she couldn't read the look in his eyes, but she hoped more than she'd ever hoped before that if hockey brought Daniel Dupree into her world, hockey would keep him here.

CHAPTER ELEVEN

There was no getting Paige off his mind. Daniel knew he should be prepping for the next group of cities on his itinerary. Somehow he'd managed to at least pack his bags for his departure tomorrow morning, but even with that simple a task, his thoughts repeatedly wandered back to the striking brunette with a tender heart and quick wit that had firmly rooted herself in a corner of his own heart.

Today was an important day for her at the winery. She'd explained about the competition, but try as he might, he'd focused on the way her eyes danced with pure excitement as she spoke passionately about the possibilities even placing could mean for the Baron Winery. Any details she may have mentioned had pretty much gone in one ear and out the other.

Having given up on getting any real work done today, he opted instead to head to the winery. See for himself why Paige was so excited. By now, he'd learned his way without need of the GPS. What did that say? Almost to the winery, he slowed as he drove past the old homestead set back from the road. A brick building with wrap around porch and boarded up windows, the old place had most definitely seen better days. More than once, Paige had lamented on what a shame whoever owned the property had not kept it up, but it was the glint of something akin to yearning in her eyes whenever they drove by that had him asking himself what stories did that old house have to tell and why didn't anyone want it?

Pulling into the parking lot and looking around, he saw fewer cars than he'd expected. Maybe he was here too early. A sign on the tasting room door declared it closed for a private event. Ignoring the sign, he cupped his eyes to see inside. Quickly, he spotted Paige bustling around and tapped the glass.

Her brow knit together with irritation, she glanced up. There was no mistaking the moment she recognized him. A smile bloomed across her face. He understood how a proud peacock must feel. His chest puffed out more than a little, knowing he'd been the one to put that smile on her face.

The latch clicked as she unlocked the door. "Hey."

"I couldn't stay away." He leaned down and gave her a quick kiss on the lips that was nothing like what he really wanted to do.

"As nice as that is to hear," she stepped aside to let him all the way in, "I'm running a bit like a chicken without a head right now."

"Then today is your lucky day." He made a gesture as if pushing up nonexistent sleeves. "As it turns out, rolling up my sleeves and getting to work is my specialty. What do you need from me?"

She cocked her head and chuckled lightly. "Surely, you have more important things to do than help me?"

"Never." He lifted his arms out to his sides. "Use me how you like."

For a moment he saw a flash of surprise in her eyes that immediately gave way to a flicker of something that made him go warm all over before she shook her head and sighed. "Honestly, I can use the help. I'm glad you're here."

She led him into the tasting room. Paper placemats sat on the bar. Someone had drawn perfectly round circles on them. "I need a glass on each circle."

"Where are the glasses?" He looked left then right.

"Behind the bar." She pointed him in the right direction as she began walking away. "I need to grab a few cases of wine from the cellar."

"I have a better idea." Shaking his head, he flashed a cheesy grin and lifting his arms and clenching his fists, flexed his muscles. "How about you show me which bottles of wine you want and I'll carry the heavy cases while you set up the glasses?"

Hiding a soft chuckle with her hand, she nodded. "Okay. Far be it from me to turn down muscle."

Once again, looking around as he headed to the cellar door, he turned to face her. "Where's your help?"

"For now, I'm afraid you're it. Fate decided today would be a good day to strike either my employees, or their kids, with a nasty bug. Siobhan and Eve are on their way, but it will take them a while and I'm already behind."

Stepping aside for her to lead the way downstairs, he followed her to a cage stacked with cases of wine.

With one hand she pulled her hair back from her face while pointing with the other. "This stack of cases needs to go behind the bar."

"Okay."

Before she rushed away, he touched her hand. "This is part of the competition?"

She nodded. "It's an ongoing one and we're the first winery in the rotation. I'm undecided if that's good or bad."

He rested his hands on her shoulders. "First or last, it won't matter. You make great wine."

A shaky smile teased at the corners of her mouth. "Thank you for your vote of confidence. I know we have good wine, very good wine, but I needed that." She inched up on her tippy toes and kissed his cheek before rushing off.

Following her, he carried the cases into the tasting room.

"How are you at opening wine bottles?" She waved a traditional cork screw in her hand.

"I've opened a few in my time." More than a few, but no point in going back in time to his early days of the game and wining and dining anything in a skirt now.

"Great." Her arm uncurled in front of him and she handed him a corkscrew. "Open two bottles from each case and put them back in the box. I'm not pouring until everyone gets here."

Daniel did as he was told, happy to be working alongside Paige. What he wasn't so sure of was how was he going to feel tomorrow when he was thousands of miles away?

The sight of Daniel at the door had set her heart dancing, and just as quickly her stomach sank when realization struck. Now was not a good time to have distractions taking her attention away from the competition. And if there was one thing that Daniel most definitely did well, it was distract her.

Despite knowing deep down that her wines were excellent, her nerves were on edge. Today would be the first of three important statewide competitions. Considered by many to be the Triple Crown in the wine industry, even placing in today's competition would be considered a very big deal.

Any misgivings she might have had about Daniel's presence quickly faded into the background. She'd been delightfully surprised at his offer—no, insistence—that he pitch in to help. Almost from the first day she'd met him he'd been nothing but thoughtful, considerate, cooperative, an all around good sport—especially when her family was involved—and now, very supportive.

Any minute now the judges would be walking through the front door. Everything was ready and looked absolutely perfect, and she had Daniel to thank. Siobhan and Eve had only just shown up, flustered and upset about an accident on I45 that had slowed them down. Each had glanced around, nodding their heads and smiling. Even they could see what a great team she and Daniel had made under less than perfect circumstances.

A hand on her back startled her out of her reverie. "Is there anything else you need?"

Staring into Daniel's eyes, she almost blurted out *what a loaded question.* "For now, all I need is for the judges to arrive and get this show on the road."

He nodded. "Okay then. What can I do during the competition?"

Siobhan and Eve had gathered near them. Paige cleared her mind and pictured the rest of the day. "I'll want you each at a different bar. This way, if the judges have questions you can answer them."

Daniel was the first to speak up. "Uh, I was thinking something more simple, like handing out hors d'ouevres or maybe clearing the bar."

Both her sisters' heads bobbed in agreement.

"He's got a point." Siobhan actually looked a bit green. "If you want to hand out some Guinness I might be of help, but wine?"

"What she said." Eve waved a thumb in their youngest sister's direction. "Except for the Guinness part."

Shaking her head quickly, Paige held up her hands. "No, no. You don't need to give the judges any information, the objective is to let them tell us what they smell and taste."

Daniel's brows pleated in thought. "So the opposite of doing a tasting."

"Right." Paige nodded. "Most of the help originally scheduled for today are fairly new and were going to need a little extra support, so there will be cue cards at your fingertips with basic information on the wine. In case the judges have any questions."

"I love cheat sheets." Daniel smiled, his hand returning gently to the small of her back.

The warmth of his touch set her slightly off balance for only a moment before she reminded herself what was at stake here. "Are you all set?"

All three heads bobbed, her nerves instantly calmed, and excitement began to hum again. This competition could put Baron Winery in the league with some of the better known Napa and Sonoma vintners. Her winery had done better than anyone had expected so far, but she wanted to grow the business and its reputation the same way she'd grown the vines.

Looking at the bar in front of them, the smile on Daniel's face slipped. "Uh, exactly where at my fingertips are these cheat sheets?"

Her gaze darted left than right. She sprinted to the next set up of glasses and muttered under her breath before spinning around to face him. "I'll be right back." She sprinted toward her office.

"How soon before the judges arrive?" Daniel followed on her heels.

"In a few minutes." Lifting papers, notebooks, and any other thing the index cards might be hiding under, she didn't bother looking at Daniel.

Completely unaware of how out of kilter she felt every time he stood close enough for her to smell his cologne, he came and stood behind her. One hand gently resting on her shoulder, the other reached around her and stretched for something poking out from under a marble cheese board she'd been using as a paperweight ever since Siobhan had done an ambiance photo shoot for them a few months ago. "Could these be what you're looking for?"

His breath warmed her neck and tickled her senses. The man really did know how to distract her. Nodding, very slowly, she actually hummed before finding her words. "Yes. Thank you."

Much to her regret, his hands fell to his sides and he took a step in retreat, followed by another. "I presume these names match the labels on the bottles?"

Almost wishing he hadn't stepped away, knowing she didn't have time for wishes, she nodded and sucked in a brain clearing breath. "Yes, it has to be simple and obvious for the employees. Are you ready?"

He lifted his gaze from the cards and took a step toward the doorway. "Don't worry. I've got your back."

All of her life, she'd known that the Baron family had her back. Though there might be a lecture or grimace attached, she could count on every one of her siblings or cousins and especially grandparents to support her. Until this very moment, it had never occurred to her that there might be a person in the world not related by blood who would have her back. She liked it. A lot. Now the question at hand, the one that threatened to drive her once again to distraction, was did he mean tonight, or from now on?

CHAPTER TWELVE

The way Paige was pining, replaying her and Daniel's time together, and missing him more than she'd expected, anyone would think he'd been gone for months, not days. As much as she loved her large, loud, and occasionally overbearing family, after eating more than she should have, a walk seemed like a great way to clear her head. She'd spent hours at the main house with everyone and yet had no idea what everyone spoke about. Her mind had been firmly preoccupied with one former hockey player.

All this missing a man was a new experience for her, and she simply couldn't decide what to make of it, or what to do about it. A part of her wanted to think that maybe he was missing her too, but another side of her knew that was unrealistic. Daniel was up to his eyeballs in final evaluations. Why would he have time to even think of her, never mind miss her? Still, every text and call ran through her mind on a never ending loop. No matter how she sliced it, none of it was the same as having him here, feeling the warmth of his hand in hers, or the gentleness of his touch when he'd steal a kiss. What was it they always said: Absence makes the heart grow fonder.

Maybe that was all it was. Or not. And here she was once again in the same back and forth conversation with herself, which was why she'd decided to step outside for some fresh air and hopefully a little perspective. She'd opted to bring her grandmother's puppies. Though they'd grown so much the last few months, they were nothing like the little fuzz balls that her brother Kyle had adopted in an effort to make a good impression on a girl, but Honey and

Moon were still young enough to have more energy than the Tasmanian Devil. At least now they followed some rules. Barely. "Y'all know you're better company than people sometimes, don't you?"

As if fully understanding and agreeing, the two dogs came to a stop at her side, plopped their rear on the ground, and sent their tails swishing.

"I know what you want." Lowering herself onto one knee. She pulled out two training treats from her pocket that her grandmother had given her. One for each dog. Gingerly, each one scooped up their treat from her hand. In return for the pups improved manners, she scratched each one's chins. "Y'all are such good listeners. The best part is, unlike my two-legged family, you don't ask any questions."

After giving the pups one last scratch, she straightened to her full height. Taking a second, she glanced down at her phone. No new texts. In only a few days she'd come to cherish their long calls and brief texts, but they were no substitute for the man himself. Indifferent to her dilemma, the dogs kept running ahead and then coming back as if to hurry her along. She rounded some fences, keeping the house in sight until she reached the barn. A light inside surprised her. She hadn't expected to find anyone working at this hour.

Studying the open door, she crouched down to love on the dogs once again while her gaze narrowed and focused on the distance. Convinced it was time to play, the pups bounced around her, pausing to come in and lick her face. Laughing and shaking her head, she firmly told the two to sit. Then, when they did as told, she rewarded them with another treat. "You may not know it right now, but y'all have an easy life."

Honey barked and she'd have sworn the other dog nodded at her.

"What are you doing here?" Mitch, the oldest of Bradley Baron's children, came walking over to where she was still squatting with the dogs.

One eye closed, she squinted up at her brother, wondering when had he slipped away from the table unnoticed. "I could ask the same of you." She pushed to her feet, dusting off her slacks.

Mitch shook his head. "Nope. I asked you first."

"Just needed some fresh air." Of all her family, Mitch was the one most likely to relate to missing someone, but she wasn't ready to share. At least not till she made a little more sense of her own feelings. Right now she felt a bit like a military wife, missing her husband and yet going on with her day pretending all was well. Her own words struck her with the force of a two by four. *Wife*? Was that what she wanted? Where she and Daniel were heading?

"Why do you look like you just stepped on a tack?" Her eldest brother tipped his head to one side, studying her. He'd always had such a quiet, pensive way about him. At least since his wife died all those years ago.

"Do you still miss her?" Paige hadn't meant to blurt it out, but there it was.

His eyes flew open and the way he took a half step back anyone one would think he'd been the one hit with a two by four.

"Sorry." She shook her head. "That's none of my business."

For a short moment, his eyes closed and she could hear the ragged intake of breath as he slowly blew it out. Once his eyes opened it was easy to see all the love and hurt inside him. Apparently so could Honey and Moon as they'd quickly abandoned her to sit at Mitch's side.

"Only every day." He patted each dog's head then looked at her. "I'm checking on a new calf, let's walk."

He led her to a stall where a calf that could only have been born hours ago, walked on shaky legs. And just like that, all the pain seemed to slip away as a smile pulled at his lips.

Paige leaned over the low railing. "This never gets old."

"I know." His gaze remained on the calf. "I'm guessing this line of questioning has something to do with our recent hockey guest?"

She nodded. Silence reigned for a short while.

"So it's serious?" His gaze remained focused on the calf

now latched to his mother's underside.

"I'm starting to think so."

Now his head turned and he looked at her. "Starting?"

"Okay. Yes. For me. I think. Maybe." She sucked in a breath and nodded her head. "Definitely. Yes."

The laugh that reached Mitch's eyes had not been the expected response. "If anyone is asking for my vote, a definite yay."

"So what do I do about it?"

"Aw, kid." His shoulders dropped, his eyes squeezed shut, and he blew out a sigh. "Sorry. Why is it so hard to remember you're all grown up?"

That made her laugh. "I feel the same way some days."

He nodded. "I can't tell you what to do. All I can say is follow your heart and don't waste any time. Every minute is precious."

Of course he was right, but… "The winery has been my whole world. I don't know if there's enough of me for my own family too."

This time Mitch shook his head. "Paige, I've watched you take a batch of wine that had no hope and turn it into a great vintage. You've taken a run down and forgotten winery and put it on the map again."

"I think wine is easier than human beings."

"That's not the point and you know it. I've never seen you walk away from a challenge. You can do anything you want. That is, if you want."

She smiled up at her brother. "I want."

Suddenly, all the floundering and confusion seemed to fade away. Mitch was right. She was a Baron, after all. And she did want Daniel and all the trappings. Very much.

Where there's a will, there's a way. Almost a family motto. And the first hurdle to overcome would be that Daniel didn't live in Houston. She didn't like the idea of a long-distance relationship. She'd tried that the last few days and didn't care for it one bit. Which meant they had to make sure the Comets moved to Houston. After all, it wasn't like she could up and move the winery to another state.

Staring down at what had now become a sprawling spreadsheet, Daniel did his best to focus on the details instead of wondering what Paige might be doing right about now. The wine competition had been frenetic, he'd been totally out of his skill set, but he couldn't have imagined being anywhere else.

None of which changed that he still had a job to do. Under different circumstances, like not spending every spare minute with a captivating brunette, he would have been better prepped for this city as well as he had been for the previous ones he'd visited. Rubbing his hand down his face, he wondered what the hell was wrong with him. He'd only been gone from Houston for two days, but it seemed like a lifetime. Talking on the phone and exchanging texts with Paige had helped make her feel closer, but not as close as being in the same room able to hold her hand, or brush a wayward lock of hair behind her ear and steal a kiss while he was at it.

He sighed and paced the room. Earlier today he'd spent hours on a video call with the committee. They'd agreed with his report narrowing the field of contenders down to only a few, Houston being in the lead. Now it was up to him to determine where, or if, these last two cities fit in the ring. Neither city had given him anything close to the same welcome as he'd received in Houston. Then again, he hadn't really expected it.

At this point he was so tired of looking at stadium sizes, finances, and fan demographics, he was ready to draw straws merely to get the entire process over and return to Texas.

His phone dinged. He glanced at the name and smiled. "Hey, Henry."

"How's the world traveler? More limousines and top-of-the-line suites? Has anyone offered you their firstborn?"

Daniel chuckled. Not their firstborn, but an unforgettable granddaughter. "No offers like that."

There was a brief pause in his brother's response. "You sound odd right now. If you're tired of being wined and dined, you could come back and hit the boards."

Intuitively, his hand dropped to rub his knee. Just thinking about actually playing hockey again made his leg ache from toe to hip. No one loved playing hockey more than he had, and for a very long time, resentment at not being able to play again had been as much of a sore spot as his injuries. Now, whether he stayed with the job he knew he loved or took the plunge to give coaching a shot, no matter how he sliced it, his hockey playing days were not coming back. "No, thanks."

"Then what's going on?" All teasing slipped from his brother's voice.

His brother knew him too well. There'd be no hiding his interest in Paige from Henry, but more importantly, Daniel didn't want to keep her to himself anymore. "I met a woman."

"I knew it. I sensed a disturbance in the force. Another groupie?"

The rush of anger that rose inside surprised Daniel. "It's not like that."

"No?"

Daniel sucked in a calming breath. "She's special."

"Does this mean that Houston is on the shortlist?"

"They have a lot to offer."

"They or she?"

"The city checks a lot of the boxes we need. Even more." Having lowered his voice the way he would when he was reproving a junior player, Daniel wasn't sure who he was trying to convince of his impartiality, his brother or himself. "The decision has nothing to do with Paige."

"Paige. Pretty name." His brother's smile came through the line as clearly as his words. "Does the rest of her match?"

"Watch it." The words came out more like a growl.

"Whoa. Take it easy." Henry paused. "Are we talking serious?"

"Maybe." He hoped more than maybe.

"Just how serious? Sharing the sheets or wedding rings and pitter patter of little feet?"

Images of his holding the hands of a toddler version of Paige as he leaned forward on skates teaching her how to walk across the ice brought a wide smile to his face.

"Holy hockey pucks. You're thinking about the whole shebang, aren't you?"

Daniel nodded as if his brother could see him. Before he could find words to explain what he was feeling, his phone clicked with another call. "It's my boss. I better answer this."

"Go, but I'm waiting for you to call back. You don't drop a bomb that you're in love and then run off."

He didn't have time to argue with his brother. The call disconnected and the phone switched to his boss. "Hello."

"Daniel. We've got some changes. This looks like it might shift those precious spreadsheets of yours."

He couldn't fathom anyone coming up with a more positive front than Houston but he nodded at the phone and braced for what it could be. "What's up?"

"Looks like someone from Salt Lake has been sleeping under your bed."

"What?" Now he wondered if the committee chair, his boss since he'd come aboard the Comets' team, had been drinking his lunch today.

"They've heard that the Barons and Houston are pulling out all the stops."

These things happened. The Comets wanting to move was no secret in the sports world.

"They've sweetened the pot. A lot."

Daniel's grip on his phone tightened and he sank onto the edge of the bed. Not till this very moment did he realize how badly he wanted Houston to win fair and square so he could make Paige happy. "What have they got?"

"The city council has approved a bond for a new stadium."

So far that didn't rock the boat. A lot of cities had promised that.

"A new light rail line has been prioritized to the top of

their infrastructure schedule, dropping passengers at the door of the new stadium."

He nodded. That was good, but not earth shattering.

"The list of tax breaks is as long as my arm. Daniel, the penny a year lease agreement for the first five years alone will be a nice chunk of change for salaries. The whole package should be in your email by now."

Way ahead of his boss, Daniel had already accessed his email and was quickly scanning the city's updated proposal. His boss wasn't exaggerating. Daniel felt the blood rushing from his head.

So far, Paige and the Barons aside, Houston was sitting pretty to win the spot despite the downside of hurricane season overlapping much of the hockey season. As of five minutes ago, they'd been bumped into second place. What was he going to tell Paige?

CHAPTER THIRTEEN

Paige couldn't be more excited to see Daniel again than a kid on Christmas morning hoping for a new bicycle. They'd talked on the phone, but she could hear a strain in his voice. At first she'd feared he'd fallen into the cliché, *out of sight out of mind*, but she quickly realized what she was hearing was the stress from the whole process.

Though she would have preferred their first encounter to have been just the two of them, he insisted on needing to speak to her and the Governor. Clearly, he had news of the teams move, but good or bad, nothing could squelch the excitement of seeing him again face to face.

Peeking between the curtains for a glimpse of his car coming down the road, she hadn't moved for some time.

"Boy, you really do have it bad." Her brother's voice carried over her shoulder.

She let go of the curtain and spun around to face him. "Shh. Someone will hear."

Like a little boy who had spilled the beans, his shoulders hunched up and his face scrunched into the cutest of apologetic expressions. "Sorry. Didn't realize it was supposed to be a secret."

Only the sound of gravel crunching outside stopped her from rolling her eyes at her brother. Just short of a full on run, she hurried to front door, swinging it open at the same moment Daniel's fingers inched toward the door bell. "Hi."

A sweet sloppy grin took over his face. "Hi."

"Oh, brother." Mitch almost groaned from behind them. "I'll be waiting for you with the Governor in his office."

Daniel closed the distance between them and before she

could get in another word, his mouth came down on hers. All the weight of her feelings had her falling hard against him. Folded in the warmth of his arms, she'd never felt more...more.

A throat cleared behind them and Paige realized that Daniel had picked her up off the floor and her legs had wrapped around his waist. They fit together so perfectly well. They were definitely meant to be.

The Governor banged his cane on the hardwood floor. "I have a meeting with the rest of the Houston committee in thirty minutes. There'll be plenty of time for reunions later."

As her grandfather walked away, she slowly slid to her feet. "Missed you."

"Ditto." His hand latched on to hers, and he leaned in for a short, sweet, and quick peck on the lips. "But we need to get moving. We don't want your grandfather sending the Marines after us."

Still holding hands, they hurried into the Governor's office and took seats beside Mitch.

"I hear the final reports are in." The Governor glanced up from his place behind the massive desk.

His expression stone-faced, Daniel nodded.

"And it's not looking good for Houston at the moment."

Daniel's expression crumpled into one of confusion.

The Governor almost smiled at Daniel's reaction, almost. "My man, one doesn't have as many years as I have under my belt without having made friends along the way."

And sadly, enemies, she thought.

Daniel nodded and straightened in his seat. "I'm afraid another city has topped Houston's tax break offer by quite a bit."

Her grandfather's narrowed gaze lingered an uncomfortable moment on Daniel. "Can we make it up?"

Daniel shrugged. "I'm not at liberty to say, sir."

That had her grandfather's brows buckling and lips pressing tight. She had no idea if there would be a solution or explosion forthcoming.

"Perhaps," Mitch leaned forward, "we could have an emergency meeting of the committee. See what else we can add to the pot quickly. Up the ante."

Tension eased from their grandfather's face. "No time for that." His gaze shifted to Daniel. "Am I correct?"

"Probably."

"That's what I thought." He paused a moment. "What if, rather than rent free, we assign ownership of our stadium to the Comets as long as they remain at least, say, ten years in Houston?"

Daniel sighed. "A stadium that by today's standards and fan demand is no longer considered a state of the art stadium, even with the updates you've done."

"Which means," Mitch leaned back again, "our competition has or will have a nice shiny new stadium and it won't cost the Comets much if any money."

The way Daniel's gaze darted from Mitch to the Governor, Paige knew he was fighting for a way to respond and remain neutral. "No comment."

"I see." The Governor looked out the window. He and everyone else in the room knew that reply was as good as a *yes*. "We need to come up with more. Fast."

Without adding a word, Daniel nodded.

The Governor began tossing out potential areas of interest from concessions to parking. None brought out the positive reaction from Daniel they were hoping to find.

"I'm afraid, sir," Daniel cupped his hands and leaned forward, "you're going to have to come up with something outside of the box."

All the excitement and delight that had been dancing inside her at the thought of a future with Daniel deflated like a ruptured balloon. Daniel's business was hockey. Even if he left the Comets franchise, his work would take him to another state with another team. Which did nothing to assuage the doubts now battling inside her. If Houston didn't win the bid for the team, if the team moved to another state, if Daniel moved to another state, if being together meant Paige moving as well—could she give up all she'd worked for? Did she love Daniel enough to give up her winery?

Daniel would have given anything for that meeting to go differently, to wipe the worry from Paige's brows and instead have reason to celebrate. Quietly, he'd followed her onto the front porch.

"I can't bear the thought of being confined in four walls right now." Paige spun around to face him. "Let's go for a ride."

"My car or yours?" They began their descent down the front steps.

"Neither. Nothing is better to lift a heavy mood than to feel the wind in your hair and far away from the big city than being on a horse. Wait." Paige stopped in her tracks.

Daniel stood stock still, unsure if she'd had a change of heart or perhaps he was about to step on a snake or something.

Her gaze shifted to meet his. "I've already almost starved you at a steak restaurant and then risked dehydration by putting you on a moving boat to upchuck the contents of your stomach. You're not allergic to horses or something, are you?"

He smiled. "No allergies."

"Good." She proceeded down the last two steps before stopping and jetting her hand out to snag his, and interlaced their fingers. "We'll take it slow till you get the hang of it."

"I'm sure I'll be fine." No point in telling her they had horses in Canada too.

The barn was a short walk from where they'd had the meeting. The outside of the structure was deceiving. He hadn't expected so much space inside. Rows of stalls, of all sizes and purposes, flanked either side. Made sense that the Barons could have a fleet of horses if they so desired.

Paige led him to a horse so black, the hair reflected the light above its head. "Meet Cabernet."

"Named after a favorite wine?" Daniel didn't bother to hide his amusement.

A sweet smile crossed her lips. The first since the less

than pleasant meeting. "Even before the Governor bought the winery, I'd been fascinated with how the French made wine."

He scratched the horse's nose. "What a beauty. Do you ride her often?"

Giving the horse a good pat on the jaw, she leaned her head against the animal and whispered, "Sorry Cab, I didn't bring you any carrots." Turning to face him, she shook her head. "Not nearly as often as I'd like." With her back to the stall, the horse moved her head, her nose at just the right height to give Paige a nudge.

Biting back a smile, Daniel reached out to scratch the horse's neck. "I don't think she's going to let you get away with no treat."

Paige took a few steps across the way to the tack room, stuck her hand in a tub and returned, handing one chunk to Daniel, and feeding the other to Cabernet. "I know it's not the same, girl, but here you go."

"She doesn't seem to mind." He watched as the horse finished nibbling on the chunk Paige had given her and then, clearly content, rubbed her head gently against Paige's shoulder.

"I know, girl. I love you too. Ready for a ride?"

To his surprise, the horse bobbed its head. "Which horse do you want me to ride?"

A grin on her face as wide as the barn, beamed at him. She pointed to the stall next door. "Get acquainted with Comet."

"Comet?" Daniel glanced at the gray gelding and back.

"Don't get too full of yourself. We've had him since long before Houston developed an interest in your hockey team. But the name's fitting, don't you think?"

Tugging Paige close, he grabbed her other hand and looking down at her, ignored what he really wanted to do and settled for kissing the tip of her nose. "I wish I could change how things are panning out, but mine isn't the final word. For what it's worth, despite everything, I do think Houston is the better choice."

"I know." Still holding onto his hands, she took a short

step in retreat. "We know it's not your fault. Don't let it worry you. We're Barons. Where there's a will, there's a way."

"From anyone else, I wouldn't hold out much hope, but from your family," he chuckled, "I just don't know."

She shrugged and let go of his hands.

Wishing he could keep her in his arms, he too stepped back, moving to the stall where Comet had stuck his head out. Holding his hand out flat in front of the curious horse, he fed him one of the tablets that Paige had given him when she'd fed Cabernet. "Hey there." The large animal snuffled at him, and he scratched his chin. "I hope this means we're going to be friends."

With the help of one of the stable employees, it hadn't taken long to have the horses saddled and ready for their riders. Daniel was tall enough that he could place one foot in the stirrup and swing himself up and over without help. Paige had done the same, Cabernet being a couple of hands shorter than Comet.

Out of the barn, and slowly walking across the dirt drive and stopping at the top of the crest, he would have sworn he could see all the way to Louisiana. The ranch name, Paradise Ridge, suited the countryside perfectly.

Paige loosened the reins, made a tsking noise with her mouth, and the horse trotted away.

Easily keeping pace, Daniel relaxed his hold on the reins and fell into step beside Cabernet. "I can't imagine having grown up on a spread like this."

"Funny, I can't imagine having spent much of my youth anywhere else."

He understood she needed a little time to make peace with the unexpected turn of events. The city of Houston, with the help of the Barons, had put an excellent bid together. It hadn't hurt any that the locals, without any influence from the family or the committee, had shown him that hockey fans were plentiful. Unfortunately, in the business world, money did most of the talking.

"You doing okay?" Paige cocked her head in his direction.

"Fine."

"You did well mounting Comet. You've ridden before?"

"A little." It had been decades since he and his brother had spent their summers at their grandfather's mountain cabin, mostly on horseback.

They'd covered a lot of rolling hills in the half hour or so since they'd left the barn. Few words were spoken, and that was fine with Daniel. For the first time ever in his life, he understood the meaning of comfortable silence. Until a rumble sounded above.

"Where did that come from?" Paige held a steady gaze, studying the black clouds rolling much too quickly in their direction.

It didn't take a genius or a great horseman to understand that out in the middle of open country, with lots of very tall trees, was no place to be with a nasty storm moving in at the speed of a jet plane. "We should probably head back, don't you think?" He couldn't imagine those heavy clouds were the kind that would roll by in a few minutes.

"Definitely." Paige turned around, pointing Cabernet toward the ranch house when a bolt of lightning zigzagged its way from a cloud to the ground.

The explosive clap of thunder that accompanied the flash of light set Cabernet into a frenzy. Rearing high on her hind legs, Cabernet left Daniel with visions of the horse sending Paige flying into the stormy air and landing on the ground in broken pieces.

"Whoa." Paige's voice echoed through the gust of wind that had made an appearance as quickly as the clouds above.

For whatever reason, Comet seemed less concerned with the storm. Typical male.

Another clap of thunder struck and the sky opened, dumping a cascade of hard rain. This time there was no reassuring the terrified horse. Despite Paige's efforts at soothing the distraught animal, Cabernet reared up again and landing hard, took off at a gallop so fast she could have won the Kentucky Derby by a mile.

He didn't care how good a horseman Paige was, in this

storm, on a scared mare, and riding like the wind, every hair on his body stood on edge. A terrifying vision of Paige falling from the horse and having a two ton beast stomp down on top of her, sent adrenaline soaring through his veins.

Kicking Comet hard with the heels of his boots, Daniel leaned forward. Fully loosening his grip on the reins, and whipping the leather straps from side to side, he hollered at the gelding to fly. Time seemed to pass in slow motion as he gained on the escaping animal ahead. His heart hammered in his chest. He had to keep her safe. *Please dear lord, don't let her fall.*

Hooves pounding hard against the firm ground beneath its feet matched the fierce rhythm of a terrified heart beat. Somehow the beast beneath him had to go faster, had to out run Cabernet. "You can do this!" he told the horse as if there were any chance he could hear, never mind comprehend. Or maybe he was reassuring himself. He couldn't lose Paige now. He couldn't.

Another nudge with his heels and Comet seemed to finally understand. The horse gave one final push against the battling wind and pulled up beside Cabernet. Keeping pace with the racing horse, Comet remained just close enough to let Daniel grab hold of the reins and pull with all his strength. The still frightened mare jerked to one side and Daniel could see the devil in her eyes. The animal was more than terrified. "Whoa," he called out over the sound of pounding rain. "Whoa," he repeated, pulling hard and calculating what were the odds of both Paige and him getting killed if he tried to leap across onto the backend of the mare.

Before he could do something as stupid as that, the frantic animal slowed. Another few seconds, another few tugs and the four of them, human and beasts, were standing still in the middle of the pouring rain, gasping for air.

"You okay?" he shouted through the rain.

Paige's chest heaved out and in as her head bobbed and her hand gripped the reins more tightly. "She's never done that before. I…" she swallowed and heaved in another deep breath, "don't know that she would have stopped without you. Thank you."

All he could do was nod. The fear of possibly losing her sent shudders through every cell of his body. He needed a few moments to get a grip. Then once they dried off, he had every intention of holding her and never letting go.

CHAPTER FOURTEEN

At the speed the horses had run, the barn was in sight not far ahead. Taking slow and even breaths to steady her still pounding heart, they took their time, despite the rain, to head for home. The entire time, Paige practically hugged Cabernet's neck, murmuring reassuring words into the horse's ear. Though she probably needed to hear the words as much as the horse. Spotting the open barn door, both horses walked inside like a homing pigeon to its cage and came to a stop.

One of the stable hands came rushing toward them. "I was about to go find you, Miss Baron."

Paige dismounted, giving Cabernet several more reassuring strokes. "We're fine, but soaking. Take care of the horses for us, please. We just need to get to the ranch and dry off."

"Yes, ma'am, but the storm has everyone in emergency mode."

"Emergency?" Paige looked over her shoulder. "Flash floods were nothing new in Texas, but an emergency?"

"Seems that hurricane that's been sitting off the Gulf Coast has turned toward Houston. They're predicting this could make Harvey look like an afternoon shower."

"Damn." Paige turned on her heel and almost ran from the barn, waving for Daniel to follow.

Not hesitating, he turned and easily kept pace with her. "I gather this is very bad news?"

"I know what you're thinking. This, hurricanes, is exactly why the Comets had Houston at the bottom of their list."

He shook his head. "I didn't say a word."

"Doesn't matter." Not slowing down, she turned to level her gaze with his. "If the weather reports are right and a hurricane is going to hit this far north, a hockey team is the least of my worries."

Paige couldn't move fast enough. *Damn.* She did not need this. Not now.

"Paige?" Right beside her, Daniel yanked her from her thoughts. "We're not racing back to the house to get out of the rain, are we?"

Not taking her eyes off the driveway ahead, she shook her head. "The grapes. The vines."

"I was afraid you were going to say that."

"Just a few more weeks. That's all I'd need to pick the grapes" She tried to catch her breath. She, the vineyard, the winery, they were so close to reaching all her goals for this new wine. So close.

"It will be okay." At her side, Daniel snatched hold of her hand. That's all it took to ease her raising heart. Somehow, she believed him.

"I'm only stopping for a second at the house. If we're going to secure the vineyards, try to save the grapes, we're going to need extra hands." Already forming a plan of action, even though she had no idea who was still at the main house, she nodded at her own thoughts. "You'll need to get out of those wet clothes and into something dry."

"And you?"

"No time."

He shook his head and tugged at her hand till she glanced at him. "If you go, I go. You're not doing this alone."

"My brothers will—"

With a shake of his head, he cut her off. "Where you go, I go. No arguments."

For the last few minutes all she could think was that her precious grapes were still on the vine. She'd actually forgotten about the guy rushing to keep pace beside her. No, not any guy, a special guy. A great special guy.

She opened her mouth about to argue and saw the steely determined gaze staring back at her and she knew what she had to do. "Skip the house. I'll call the Governor from the road."

Again, he nodded and shifted direction toward the driveway and the cars lined in front. "My car or yours?"

"Mine's higher to the ground and we'll get better traction."

No questions asked, he continued as instructed.

She pulled out her phone, pressing at the screen. "Losing the grapes now would set me back for the year. There are reserves still in the tank, but not enough to get through the year if the crop is lost."

"Hell, that's worse than I thought." He seemed to walk a little faster.

Her grandfather's voice came through the phone. "You coming in from out of the rain?"

"We've got trouble."

"What kind of trouble?" the former governor asked in his commanding voice.

"I need to get to the winery before the wind begins to kick up even further. I could use some extra hands."

"We'll meet you there." The call disconnected.

There was no doubt in her mind that her grandfather was right now rallying the troops and she'd have plenty of hands to help. What she didn't know was—even rushing like the wind—did she have enough time?

What Daniel really wanted to do right now was take this woman in his arms, run his fingers through those beautiful locks and keep her there until all was right with the world. Unfortunately, he'd have to keep his druthers to himself and do whatever he could to help save her dream.

Key fob in one hand, Paige slipped the phone into her pocket and yanked at the door handle. Her fingers slipped, mostly from the rain, partly from the nerves that no doubt coursed through her beside the sheer determination he'd grown to love.

When she muttered a curse that would make a Marine blush, he almost chuckled. Instead, he reached around her and pulled the door open for her. Wasting no time, he ran around the hood and climbed into the passenger seat. Latching his seatbelt in place, he looked up at her. "If I've learned anything about the Barons, it's that you are a force of nature all your own."

In a hurry or not, she leaned in and gave him one quick kiss. "Thank you. Nothing else could have made me feel even a little better, and you just made me feel a whole lot better. I guess I needed to be reminded."

"Don't forget, I'll always have your back." With the grace of God, he hoped to prove that to her for the rest of their lives.

The corners of her mouth tipped up and the strength in her eyes gave way momentarily to an appreciative sparkle before battle mode returned, and turning the ignition, she put the car in gear.

The good thing about the Baron family cars was that even the utility vehicles could fly at the hand of the right driver. Despite the rain, she made it to the winery in record time. Already he could see the vineyard was a buzz of activity. "Looks like your employees are getting a head start."

"Guess I'm surrounded by great people." She smiled at him and he had to fight that urge to yank her to his side and kiss her silly.

The rain was coming down in sheets, and the wind was picking up even more. Ugly black clouds made it feel like the last moments of dusk. How the hell were they going to pull this off?

Sensing from her stance that she had to be thinking the same thing, he squeezed her hand. "You got this."

Squeezing back, she muttered, "We've got this."

"We," he repeated softly. That was a word he was going to learn to like a lot. Together they hurried to the vines where the workers had begun tying things down more securely.

"We need the netting!" Her voice could hardly be heard

through the wind.

"I'll get it!" Daniel shouted. "Where is it?"

"Storage shed next to the tank room." She surveyed the rows of vines, then glanced over her shoulder in the direction of the tank room. "I'd better come with you. Only way to protect the grapes is to get the vines wrapped."

Against the wind, Paige ran faster than Daniel would have expected. He stayed on her heels.

As they rushed up the slope, Paige shouted at him, "There's no doubt my people know what they were doing, this wasn't their first hurricane. But with absolutely no warning, they'd had no time to prepare. I don't even know if we have enough supplies on hand to salvage the entire crop."

"We'll figure it out." At least he hoped they would. Saving the grapes mattered more to him than he would have expected. He understood, from now on, what mattered to Paige, mattered to him.

Pelts of rain were coming down so hard, Paige wiped the water away from her face in an angry stroke. "At this rate we might not need a hurricane to ruin my crop." Crossing the last few feet to the door in one long stride, she yanked at the door. Nothing. Banging the wooden door with her hip, hard, she tried again. "Crap."

"Let me." Daniel moved in front of her and turning the handle he gave it a slight wiggle, lifted up and pulled.

Muttering a soft thanks, she rushed past him. The place was less organized than he'd expected, and from the way she stopped short and blinked, he suspected she was just as surprised. Her gaze darted from left to right and then she pointed to the back wall. Rolled up in bundles, the black netting was piled high. "There."

There was just one problem, enough junk had been packed in front of the netting to slow down a charging bull. Too bad it wasn't enough to slow down a hurricane. Frantically shoving boxes and other items aside as fast as they could, Daniel climbed over the last mound of crap and started hauling down the bundles. Paige was in full command mode, but he could see the worry deep in her eyes. And he didn't like it.

"Put 'em here." She'd pulled what looked like a flat furniture dolly in front of him. With the winds blowing as hard as they were, he had his doubts that the hole bunch wouldn't topple over, but it was better than running them down to the vines one at a time.

"There should be zip ties too." Her gaze darted around the piles of bundled netting.

"Here they are." Daniel held them up then spotted some bungee cords hanging from one of the racks on the side wall. "We'll secure the bundles with these."

"Great idea!" she shouted over the wind outside. "When we get all this to the vines, we'll connect one corner to the pole at the end of the row, then unroll it around and back."

"Got it!" He actually had no idea what she was talking about, but hoped it would be obvious when he got there. He might not be a vintner, but he knew time was running out.

CHAPTER FIFTEEN

From where Paige stood at the storage room door, she could already see her brothers, who had still been at the ranch when she sent out the SOS, had arrived in trucks loaded with plywood and were hammering the sheets up to protect the exposed glass. So worried about the grapes, it hadn't even occurred to her to protect the building.

Bless her Uncle Oliver's sons, Derrick and Trevor were running rope lines from the building to the vineyard. Moving against the wind was growing more and more difficult, that would be a huge help.

She could barely hear the sounds of car door after car door slamming. The footsteps stomping across a parking lot already six inches under water were silenced by the angry winds.

"Where do you want us?" Her cousins Devlin, Cameron and Leah stood in front of her wearing wading boots and rain gear. She couldn't decide if they looked like a fisherman for a fried fish commercial or the character from an old salt commercial. Either way, she had never been happier to see so many of her family coming to her aid.

"Follow us to the vines! My team are already pairing up with family and spreading out!" She was shouting as loud as she could and she could tell her family was struggling to hear. Car doors continued to slam shut and she could see more people dashing across the parking lot. The Governor must have sent off flairs. If things weren't so dire, she might have laughed.

Arms waving people on, her cousin Leah turned, leaned in, and cupped her mouth to be better heard. "You go on!

I'll send newcomers your way!"

She really didn't have time but she couldn't help reaching out and hugging her cousin before running after Daniel, Devlin and Cameron. The only sibling missing from that branch of the Baron family tree was their sister Olivia.

In Paige's business, rain was a necessary evil, but this was insane. As hard as it was already blowing, the wind picked up even more. And now the rain began to fall horizontally. That was *so* not a good sign. Things were getting worse and for everyone's safety she needed to get them inside sooner than later.

Taking up a position by a row of vines, she shouted at Daniel, "I'll hold the end! You staple it to the post!" Despite holding on as tightly as she could, the wind snatched the black netting out of her hands.

With the reflexes of a goalie, Daniel stretched out his hand and caught it. "Let me hold it." He handed her the stapler. "You put in the staples."

Smart man. His grip was stronger than hers. She needed to remember with a man like Daniel in her life, she didn't need to always do the hard parts. He would be a true partner in every sense. Moving along the row as fast as they could in the miserable conditions, she ignored her hair whipping in her face as they worked. All that mattered was to protect these grapes at all costs.

"Is this netting enough to do the job?" Daniel yelled through the whistling wind.

"It has been before. It's all we've got!"

His gaze lifted to the tall cypress pines that surrounded the building and edges of the fields of grapes. "Are they supposed to bend like that?"

Paige shook her head. Trunks the size of a telephone pole and just as tall, if not taller, with branches of pine needles clustered at the top were most definitely not supposed to bend.

"Don't worry. We'll save the grapes." He looked up a moment. "And hopefully the trees." That he was all in on saving the grapes warmed her heart. He could have been hunkered down in a comfortable hotel room, warm and dry.

Instead he was here helping her. When the wind died and rain passed, she could wrap that thought around her like a warm blanket.

The blasted net was giving them fits. "This isn't working!" she shouted. "Let's unroll the netting along the row and attach it to each pole as we go."

Daniel nodded, still wrestling the wind and the netting while Paige followed along behind him. When they reached the next pole she could see it wobble. Half as wide around as a cypress tree and about six feet tall, she needed these suckers to stay upright or her grapes wouldn't stand a chance.

She stapled the netting while Daniel held the pole steady, and prayed the blasted hurricane would take a sudden shift and just go away. Glancing around, she could barely see a dozen yards ahead, but she could tell her staff and family were making progress. Slow like her and Daniel, but progress was progress.

Daniel was ahead with his long strides despite the weather and his burden. She caught up just as the next pole looked as if some invisible person was trying to tug it from the ground. "Is that going to stay stable?" he shouted.

"It has to. I have no way of fixing it now."

Despite the wave of wind, he straightened to look down field at the work left to be done, and probably evaluating how much could they depend on those poles doing their job. Deciding something only he knew, he bobbed his chin, turned to survey the rest of the fields and then, his gaze lifting, his eyes went wide and large as a silver dollar. Hands cupping his mouth, he took off at a fast pace for someone running in mud, screaming, "Craig! Heads up!"

Her heart slammed against her chest, she tried to see what he saw. Craig and Mitch were working together several yards over. She didn't understand. Lifting her gaze, her heart stuttered to a stop at the sight of a nearby cypress teetering like a drunken sailor. Worse, looking down she could see the fallow roots tugging out of the ground. "Oh my God. Daniel!" she screamed as loud as she could and took off running, her heavy boots slipping and sliding in the

Texas clay that normally passed for dirt, and had turned to mush.

The pelting rain had become almost blinding. Waving her arms, she tried to warn everyone else to get out of the way. The tree was ready to break free. If it landed straight ahead, it would take out at least one row of grapes, but she suddenly didn't give a rats ass about the grapes or the vineyard. Craig and Mitch were in its path.

A crack louder than lightening striking snapped and the tree hung at a terrifying angle. Knowing the damn tree was going to give way, literally any second, she struggled to see ahead, spotting Daniel, arms stretched, reaching forward and shoving her brothers with all his might. A breath of relief filled her lungs as the two men seeing the tree Daniel pointed to, turned and ran. They were safe, they'd be safe.

Another snap filled the air and the tree finally gave way, the wind blowing the slow motion fall not straight ahead but to the side. The side where Daniel stood. Recognizing the shift in the tree, he turned and slogged through the mud away from the slowly falling tree's new path.

She couldn't breathe. Just as suddenly as the tree had snapped, Daniel was down on the ground. The thunder of a heavy tree slamming to the ground echoed around her. She couldn't see him. "Daniel!" tore from her throat.

Everyone was running as best they could toward the fallen tree, the grapes forgotten. No sign of movement. No sign of Daniel. He had to be okay. He had to. If he lost his life over her stupid grapes, she'd never forgive herself. Running as fast as she could, she lifted her eyes to the dark angry skies. *Dear lord. Please.*

Hurricane force winds had nothing on a falling tree. Squinting at the pouring rain, Daniel lifted an arm and moving his fingers, was delighted to see all five worked. Less than ten feet away, the bark of a lone cypress pine laughed at him. Covered in mud from hair to toe, he didn't know if he should laugh back or grab an axe and hack at the offensive trunk.

"Daniel!" Paige's panicked voice echoed between the raindrops.

Damn it. He needed to get up. Let her see he was all right. Slowly rolling to one side to push himself up and out of the muddy mess beneath him, a pain rattled between his ears. All right might have been over eager. Alive would have to do.

"Daniel!" A hundred and twenty pounds of worried female flew at him, sending him once again flat on his back. "Talk to me. Are you alive?"

The way her hands rubbed up and down his arms and caressed his face, he almost didn't want to admit he was mostly just fine. "That's an affirmative."

"Oh, thank God."

He didn't get a chance to say a word, not about the tree, the grapes, the hurricane or her family. Her lips descended on his with almost the same force as the winds knocking the grapes and trees around. And that was just fine with him. His arms curled around her and he pulled her down into the mud with him.

"Excuse me." Mitch stood over them. "Do you think you two could pick this up after the hurricane passes and we save what's left of the grapes?"

The grapes. The vineyard. A starting gun at the Derby couldn't have gotten Daniel on his feet faster. Still holding Paige with one arm, he practically yanked her upright. "How much damage did the tree cause?"

"Not much," Mitch shook his head, "thanks to that gust of wind. Forecast says the storm is finally moving east of here, but no telling how soon that'll be, and we have work to do."

Daniel nodded and ignoring the harried moments of the last few minutes, everyone got back to work, battling the wind and rain, and protecting the grapes as best as humanly possible. By the time they reached the final row of grapes to tend to, Paige had sent her family and most of her staff to seek shelter inside the winery. The last zip tie in place, the winds still howling with enough force to knock them both over, they held hands and hurried back to the tasting room.

Inside the place was pitch black, lit only by candles and glass hurricane lamps.

"Good thing I collect hurricane lamps." Paige squeezed his hand. "And keep them filled with colored lamp oil."

"Smart lady."

"I'd be smarter if I'd installed a generator. It's on the list but, didn't seem so important. Until now."

"You two need to dry off." Mitch handed them each a towel. "No idea why you have a closet filled with towels but we're all grateful."

"Wine is a dirty business." Paige shrugged.

Mitch nodded. "Good thing. Dry off then go stand by the heat vents to warm up."

"We raided your fridge." On the floor, surrounded by cousins—some he recognized, some he didn't—Siobhan held up a plate of cheese and grapes. "I should visit more often."

The cousin he did remember, Leah, lifted a box of crackers. "These are delicious. They go great with the white cheddar cheese."

"Where did you get all these varieties of cheeses?" Devlin, the cousin who seemed as much a brother as Paige's siblings, held up a piece. "And this is great. What is it?"

"That's either Saint Marcelin goat cheese or brie." Paige squinted at her cousin. To Daniel it was white and sort of gooey. "There's a cheese shop in Memorial. We place special orders for French cheeses."

"I'm with Siobhan," Devlin's brother nodded, "we need to visit more often."

"That or the cheese shop." Leah grinned.

"Don't worry." Her sister Eve walked up with a plate overflowing with cheese, crackers, and he suspected some sort of dry salami. "We saved some for you."

"Listen…" Siobhan sprang to her feet. "I don't hear the wind."

Closest to the front door, Craig unlocked the latch and with Kyle at his side, eased the door open. A moment later it swung fully open. "How about that. Sun's out."

Everyone else ran to the door and out onto the cement sidewalk. Left alone inside, Daniel turned to face Paige. "I'm sorry I scared you earlier, but when I saw that tree about to come down and knew your brothers couldn't hear me and were focused on the grapes..." he shrugged. "I had to let them know."

Paige raised her finger to his lips. "My grapes, my fault. But I am very glad you're all right."

He pulled her into the circle of his arms. "More than all right now."

"Listen." She sucked in a deep breath. "I need to say something."

His thumb caressed her jaw line. "I love you."

"Yes." Her eyes flew open wide. "How did you know I was going to say that?"

Chuckling softly, he shook his head. "No. I'm saying, I love you."

"Oh." She smothered a smile. "Well, I love you too."

"Isn't that nice." His lips came down on hers and his heart beat a rapid tattoo. Beyond any doubt, he knew for sure, this was where he belonged.

CHAPTER SIXTEEN

Cradling a warm mug of hot chocolate, Paige stood outside the tasting room, surveying her vineyard. Her intact vineyard. She owed that to her family. That her family was intact was most definitely thanks to Daniel. Any time she thought of him, she couldn't help but smile.

Once again, she took in the pristine rows of vines. Yes, a few were a bit sparse of leaves here or there, but their hurried hard work had paid off. The grapes had been saved.

It had taken several days to clean up the horrendous mess that Hurricane Mia had left behind. The netting was gone, along with every evidence that a hurricane had blown by. Fallen branches from what Paige thought had to have been every tree within fifty miles. The massive cypress pine that by mere inches had spared her vines—and Daniel—had been cut and stacked by the rear of the winery. Next winter it would burn in the fireplaces both here and at the ranch. Debris from who-knew-where even included a bicycle or two. She suspected there were a couple of kids in the Houston area who would never again leave their bikes on the front lawn. And lesson learned, a natural gas generator was on order.

There was only one order of business still unresolved. If the old adage, *no news is good news* held true, then Houston would win the bid for the Comets and the man she loved would be here full time. Technically, the future of the hockey team was still up in the air, but a girl could hope.

Daniel's car pulled into the driveway. A morning routine she'd become accustom to. Even though they spoke every night on the phone, and sent a text every morning, he also brought her coffee, and if she gave any hint of being hungry, breakfast too. Once again a smile curved the edges of her mouth.

A car she didn't recognize turned into the parking lot just behind him. Her employees were expected to filter in soon, but the tasting room wasn't due to open for another hour. Her smile gone, she eyed the car with curiosity. Were they with Daniel? Could it be more people from the relocation committee? No, that made no sense. If they went anywhere it would be the ranch.

Parked away from the door, Daniel bounded out of his car. His brows buckled with the same curiosity she had, his head cocked in the direction of the other car. "Expecting early visitors?"

She shrugged and shook her head. "Not that anyone told me."

Daniel moved in to stand by her, his hands gently on her arms, he leaned over and whispered in her ear, "That kiss I'd been looking forward to all morning is going to have to wait until we don't have an audience."

Just like that, her smile was back and threatening to take over her face. She really did love this man.

Two men in suits climbed out of their car. Who wore suits to go wine tasting? In Houston no less. "They look official."

"Mm." Daniel inched closer to her, his gaze fixed on the two men slowly crossing the parking lot.

"Paige Baron?" One of the men extended his hand.

With a nod, she accepted the proffered hand. "How may I help you?"

The man's attention shifted to Daniel. It took everything in her not to sigh and roll her eyes as they sized each other up the way men sometimes do. "I'm Carl Rawles." He waited a beat as if his name should have been known to her. "With the Wine Association Award Committee."

Wine Association? Her heart leaped in her chest as she told herself not to over react. It could be anything. Including bad news. But Daniel's hand on her back helped to keep her cool and collected. "Nice to meet you."

He introduced his companion, but Paige was far less interested in who they were than in why were they here.

"The comments about your vintages were impressive."

Impressive. That was good wasn't it? Or was that like *interesting*—what you say to a woman when you don't want to outright tell her that her new dress reminds you of your aging grandmother.

The other man nodded. "Everyone raved about them."

Raved was good. She relaxed just a tiny bit.

"Normally, you'd receive an official email."

She cast a sideways glance in Daniel's direction, curious to see if he was finding this as weird as she was.

"Since we missed the competition here, we wanted to taste your wines."

Suddenly she had an urge to ask for identification. She could hear every one of her brothers asking who shows up an hour before opening to taste wine? Maybe they were burglars. She did have some very expensive wines. Then again, what burglars wore suits?

"So," the second man extended his arms and handed her a box, "we wanted to come in person to give you your awards."

Her stomach dropped to her feet. "Awards?" *Plural?*

"Your Cabernet won gold."

She did a silent fist pump and grinned as Daniel's hands moved to her shoulder and gave a quick squeeze. She'd hoped her Cabernet would place, but gold? She desperately wanted to do a jig.

"Your Riesling, Tempranillo and Zinfandel all won silver. You placed in more categories than any other winery in the region." The man pointed to the box. "All of the medals are in there."

She'd gone from wanting to do a jig to hoping her knees wouldn't give out on her. *Any other winery.* Wow. "I can't believe you delivered them in person."

She'd swear the first guy blushed.

"Well, like I said, normally you'd just get an email and the awards would be sent shortly thereafter, but we really did want to taste the wines."

Daniel squeezed her shoulders again and she realized the men were waiting for her to offer them a taste. "Sorry. Let's go pour you some wine."

She waited for the men to go inside then spun around to face Daniel, holding the door open. She did a very tiny jig in place, let out the softest squeal, and then kissed him on the tip of his nose. Could this day get any better?

Daniel stood in the doorway behind Paige, waving mindlessly at the two men who had walked out the door. Not until they had started their cars and driven out of the parking lot did Paige stop waving.

Slowly her hand dropped to her side. When she spun around and squealed so loud he was pretty sure the two men now speeding down the freeway could have heard her. "I won!" Throwing her arms around him, she squeezed him tightly, still squealing softly.

Caught up in the moment, he lifted her off the ground and spun her around. "I told you before and now there's proof: you make great wine."

Her smile settled into sweet contentment. "I do, don't I?"

Spinning her around again, he captured her lips against his and kissed her for much less time than he wanted. Pulling his head back, he leveled his gaze with hers. "What do you say we let the afternoon crew handle the tourists and go celebrate?"

"I think that's a great idea, but I need to make one stop first."

"The ranch." It wasn't a question. He'd come to learn how close this family was, and if he'd had any doubts, the way every single cousin within a twenty mile radius traveled through hurricane winds to come to Paige's aid, there wasn't a single doubt now.

It had taken Paige less than five minutes to accept her staff's congratulations for the umpteenth time, and let them know she'd be gone the rest of the day. Clay assured her they could handle whatever came up.

"Are we sure the Governor is home?" Daniel asked as they pulled onto the ranch road.

Paige nodded. "Sent Grams a text. They're home."

They had barely made it halfway up the front steps when the door opened and the two puppies bolted outside to greet them. A few feet behind the dogs, the Governor banged his cane on the wooden floor and both dogs dropped their rears on the spot. Tails swishing like crazed brooms. Another tap of the cane and both pups trotted into the house. Definitely progress.

"Perfect timing. I was just going to give you a call."

"I have news." Paige beamed as she trotted passed her grandfather into the house.

"As do I." The older man followed them indoors. "Let's go into my office."

"I want Grams to hear too."

"Grams is here." The sweet woman who had reigned over this large brood appeared in the doorway. "What has you effervescing like a shaken bottle of seltzer?"

A fraction more composed than when she'd squealed earlier, twice, Paige grinned widely. "The Cabernet won gold in the wine competition I entered."

Her grandmother scooped her into her arms for a congratulatory hug. "That's wonderful news." Mrs. Baron turned to where her husband stood by his desk. "Isn't it, dear?"

The old guy looked as stern as a high school principal, but even Daniel could see the pride in his eyes. "Yes, it is. Well done."

Without batting an eye, Paige eased out of her grandmother's embrace and hurried across to give her grandfather a quick hug. The former Marine held her tightly for a long moment and, Daniel decided, definitely proud.

Taking a step in retreat, the Governor sank into the leather chair behind his desk. "And I have news too."

Everyone took a seat in front of the massive oak desk and waited for what came next.

"Houston has withdrawn its bid to be home to the Comets."

Sitting beside Daniel, Paige gasped. "Governor?"

Daniel had not held out much hope that Houston could out do the top bid, but he'd not totally given up yet. With every day that passed and no announcement had come, he'd thought maybe things would work out. Now, there wasn't a chance in hell. His only chance of remaining close to Paige was to convince the owners to let him work from Houston, or find a new job. There was no other option, he'd made too many plans and they all included Paige and Houston.

"No disrespect intended, Daniel, but sometimes the only way to get what you want is to go straight to the top."

Daniel nodded. "No offense taken." Besides, he had a stake in all this and wanted the Comets to come to Houston as much as the Barons did.

"There was no room for negotiation. Your boss is one tough cookie. Houston did the best they could, but the other offers were too hard to beat." The Governor shrugged. "We simply could not compete on their levels."

"Houston was willing to throw in a new rink, but your park and rides were no match for a new light rail system." As much as Daniel hated to admit it, there was no point in sugarcoating the situation.

"Our only option was to change strategies." The Governor actually smiled.

Daniel knew the man was a former Marine officer so strategy should be his strength, but hockey and war were two different things. Usually.

The Governor leaned forward and steepled his fingers. "Daniel."

"Yes, sir."

"Did you know that your boss is only a forty-nine percent owner of the Comets?"

He shook his head. "There had never been mention of another owner or partner."

Grinning like the cat who ate the canary, the Governor leaned back again. "The majority ownership belongs to his wife."

"Really?" That was a well kept secret.

"And more interesting, apparently Mrs. Majority Owner wants to spend more time traveling and with the grandkids."

A feeling deep in the pit of Daniel's stomach was shouting for him to lean back, put up his feet, and watch a genius at work.

"I did the only thing left."

Yep. Daniel was as sure of what the Governor was going to say next as he was that he was going to marry Paige and spend the rest of his life raising little Barons.

"I bought the team."

"You what?" Paige almost fell off her seat.

"Well, the final paperwork isn't signed yet, but the preliminaries are all worked out and the deal is as good as sealed."

Daniel couldn't hold back a chuckle. Paige had warned him that Barons always got what they wanted. He had no idea if the Governor actually wanted a hockey team that badly or just hated losing that badly, but either way, he would remember never to underestimate Paige or her family again.

"Let's move this little celebration to the other room." The Governor stood, extended his elbow to his wife, and quietly exited the room.

Paige had made it less than a foot when he snagged her hand and whirled her around.

Looping his arms around her, he pulled her in even closer. "You know what this means?"

"I'm going to have to get used to having you around?" she teased.

He bobbed his head. "Are you okay with that?"

Her arms lifted to wrap around his neck. "Very." On tiptoe, she nudged his head lower until her lips met his, ending the sweet kiss much too soon. Taking a step toward the door, her hand now laced with his, she gave a tug. "They're waiting for us."

Happy to follow, his mouth curled up in a contented grin. From where he stood, it looked like the Duprees were also about to get everything they'd ever wanted.

EPILOGUE

Life as a member of the Baron family was definitely more interesting than most families. At least that's what Siobhan thought. Some days were more rewarding than others, some more stressful, but today fell under the umbrella of uniquely interesting. Somehow—though she still hadn't wrapped her head around how it had happened—the Barons now owned a professional ice hockey team.

Today, a good chunk of the clan had gathered for the groundbreaking on the new arena. Of course, the key family players involved in bringing hockey to Houston stood behind the massive blue ribbon and bow. Her grandfather, the former governor of the great state of Texas, her eldest brother the senator, her sister Paige's boyfriend, Daniel Dupree—former hockey star and new goaltending coach of the Houston Comets—and of course the mayor, and a passel of city council, and other committee members all grabbing their fifteen minutes of fame.

Despite the crowd, the two people Siobhan had her eyes on were Daniel and her sister Paige. Of course Daniel had his eye on the photographers and reporters as they held the ribbon for the Governor to cut, but those same eyes kept darting over to where Paige stood with the rest of the family. Not just any glance, his eyes sparkled enough to light a path on the darkest of Irish nights. And her sister was no exception. The sheer adoration in both their gazes was enough to make Siobhan stomp her feet and whine until a man who looked at her that way came into her life. Of course, traveling back and forth across the globe did nothing to encourage a relationship, and if she were honest with herself, not having a steady guy yet wasn't really such a bad thing. She liked playing for a living. Going to fast paced races, exotic locations, and using her photographs to bring a new light to whatever caught her fancy. Didn't hurt that it paid nice money too. Paige was a few years older, maybe waiting a little while for the right man would make more sense. There were an awful lot of decades left in her life to exchange doe-eyes with the opposite sex.

"If you keep staring at your sister, someone's going to think you're jealous." Her cousin Cooper spoke softly so no one else would hear.

Good at deflection, she raised a brow at him. "Which sister?" After all, Eve and her husband were here and looked equally besotted as Paige and Daniel. Though, they weren't staring hearts at each other from across the empty construction site.

"Nice try." Cooper shook his head and barely rolled his eyes.

Rachel leaned into her cousin. "You're not letting the secret out?"

This time Cooper did roll his eyes at his kid sister. "No, but you may have."

From the way Rachel squeezed her eyes and blew out a hiss, Siobhan was pretty sure her cousin would kick herself if she could. As a fellow baby sister with older brothers—brothers who didn't hesitate to point out an error that anyone could have made even if they weren't the baby of the family—Siobhan felt for her cousin.

Rachel held up her hand and shook her head. "I haven't said a thing."

In an effort at solidarity, Siobhan nudged her cousin. "And I didn't hear a word."

"Good. Better keep it that way, at least for a few more hours."

A few more hours? So what did her cousins the engineer and the restoration architect know that she didn't know? Her attention returned to Daniel and Paige. The ribbon cutting ceremony over, the two fell into each other's arms as if not doing so would make breathing impossible.

Now instead of wondering if she really wanted a relationship like her siblings that made her heart go all soft and mushy, she wanted to know if the secret that Cooper and Rachel knew had anything to do with the newest pair of love birds. Siobhan's gaze switched to where her cousins had gone, Rachel held a large roll of paper, probably architectural drawings, and was shaking them at Cooper. Yep, something was up, and she had no desire to wait hours to find out.

Making her way through the crowds now crisscrossing the construction site to reach their cars, she lost sight of Cooper and his sister among the throngs of onlookers. At least all the Barons in attendance, and a few who couldn't make it, would be gathering at the ranch.

Even taking it slow, by her standards, she made it to the ranch in record time. She was halfway up the front steps when her sister called out.

"Wait up." Hand in hand, Paige and Daniel trotted up to her. "We should have shared a ride."

Siobhan shrugged. She liked driving her little MINI Cooper. Besides, there wasn't a whole lot of comfortable room for extra people. Especially ones as tall as Daniel or her brothers. "Next time."

"We'd better not be breaking ground on any other sports arenas." Paige chuckled. "Hockey is about all I can handle learning."

Daniel smiled and casually lifted their laced fingers to kiss the back of her hand. And once again Siobhan's thoughts shifted back to a guy who loved her like that would be nice. She really did need to make up her mind.

"There y'all are." Devlin stood at the open front door. "The Governor has been waiting for y'all to get this little party started."

"How the heck did he beat us here?" Paige hurried up the steps.

Devlin laughed. "Who do you think we all inherited the need for speed from?"

The man had a point. Intent on finding Cooper and Rachel and getting to the bottom of the *secret*, Siobhan hurried into the main house. Sometimes she forgot just how large the Baron clan was. With six siblings of her own, their spouses or soon to be spouses, plus twenty-one first cousins, assorted aunts and uncles, and a few added close friends who might as well be family, some gatherings were more like a convention than family meal. Though the entire family was not here today, the den and veranda were packed nonetheless.

Finally, she spotted both Cooper and Rachel off to one side of the sprawling rear terrace. The two were focused ahead. Siobhan maneuvered her way through the people, pausing only for the required howdy-dos and scattered hug or kiss before coming close enough to her cousins to see what they were watching.

As close as she could tell, there was something going on inside. In one last hurried push, she made it right up beside the two who were smiling like fools and staring into their grandfather's library. "Someone announcing winning lottery numbers."

Her cousins spun around, their eyes as wide as a couple of kids caught with their hands in the cookie jar. "Shh…" Rachel put her finger to her lips.

Siobhan moved closer, sidling up beside her cousin. She had a birds eye view of the library, her sister Paige, and Daniel, and if she focused, she could hear them as well.

"So what is so all fired important for me to look at that we had to leave the party outside?" The love in Paige's eyes, and the smile on her lips, softened her words.

Daniel kissed Paige on the tip of her nose and un-scrolled a long roll of paper.

"Is that the—"

"Shh…" both her cousins sounded.

"Obviously, now that I'm staying in Houston, I need a long term place to live."

Paige nodded and glanced at the papers sprawled open on the massive desk. "More arena plans?"

"Not exactly." He took in a deep breath. "Do you remember that boarded up house on the way to the winery?"

Once again, Paige nodded. "You mean the red brick

mission style with all weeds growing over it?"

"That's the one."

"Do you know how every time we drive by you have something to say about what a shame that no one kept it up?"

"Well, it is a shame. I bet that house has great bones. With a little loving attention, it could be a wonderful house."

Siobhan leaned into Cooper. "Does this have anything to do with the secret you mentioned?"

"This is the secret. Now shh."

"I took your cousin Rachel out there a couple of weeks ago to look around."

"Trespassing?" Paige teased.

Daniel shrugged. "I'm neither confirming nor denying."

That had Paige laughing. "Talk about cover your ass."

"Yeah, well, after we walked around, she agreed with your assessment. Great bones. So with a little help from Devlin, I tracked down the owners."

Now Paige's eyes were sparkling with interest, and Siobhan would guess anticipation.

"They're asking a very reasonable price."

"Really?" Paige looked back at the papers on the desk then up to him. "So these are—"

"Drawings Rachel whipped up for me. Preliminary only. They'd need final approval."

Her gaze turned back to the pages, leaning over she fingered some of the designs. "These are great. What do you need for final approval?"

Fumbling in his pocket, Daniel pulled out a black velvet box.

Siobhan had to slap her hands over her mouth to stop the delighted gasp from revealing the couple had three voyeurs.

Even Rachel's jaw dropped to the floor. "He didn't say he was going to propose," she whispered.

For Siobhan's liking, Cooper was awfully quiet. Suddenly he dragged his eyes away from Paige and Daniel long enough to notice both Rachel and Siobhan glaring at him. "What? So I might happen to know Eve helped him pick out a ring."

Only the need for utter silence stopped Siobhan from growling at the man.

Finally, after willing her to speak, Paige looked up from the blueprints. Her gaze went from eye level down to where Daniel rested on one knee, the open box in his hand. Just like Rachel, her jaw fell, and like Siobhan, Paige's hand flew to her mouth.

"I've practiced this a thousand times a day, every day, ever since I decided, no matter what happened with the team, I couldn't go back to living without you. Will you be my wife and share my life and home?"

Paige stared, not a word coming out of her mouth.

"Lord love a duck," Siobhan muttered. "Hurry up and say yes."

"If you don't like the house, we can buy another one, or rent, or—"

His words were cut off when Paige threw herself at him, knocking them both off their feet and onto the floor. If she said anything, Siobhan didn't hear it, but judging from the way she kissed his mouth, his cheeks, his nose and back to his mouth, Siobhan took a wild guess. "I think that's a yes."

"For a second there I thought we all got it wrong," Cooper said.

"Of course not." Rachel shook her head at her brother. "Any fool can see those two are crazy about each other."

"All right." Siobhan might be the youngest of the crowd, but apparently she was the only one with any sense. A hand at each cousin's back, she nudged them away from the window. "Let's get out of here and let them have a little privacy."

"Don't I get to see him slip the ring on her finger?" Rachel asked over her shoulder.

"No," Siobhan and Cooper echoed.

When Rachel gave her brother a sharp glare, he shrugged. "What can I say, the kid is right."

Oh how she hated it when her family referred to her as a kid. She could probably grow old, collect social security, and they'd still call her kid. Had she been the one on the receiving end of a marriage proposal, they'd probably step in and insist not until she was thirty-five or fifty. She didn't have to worry about whether she wanted a good man like her sisters, her family would never let anyone within a hundred feet of her.

Glancing over her shoulder at the library window, she couldn't help but think: and wasn't that a damn shame.

Enjoy an excerpt from
Just One Shot

"Is it always this hot in Texas?" Siobhan's friend and former college roommate, Bridget waved her hand in front of her face. As if that was actually going to help.

Her gaze fixed ahead, Siobhan didn't bother to look up. "You've heard the expression, fry an egg on the sidewalk?"

Squinting at the sunlight, Bridget nodded.

"Texas invented it."

"I think next time I visit, I'll pick a cooler month."

Her camera centered on a baby bird pecking at the dirt under a scraggly shrub, Siobhan snapped the shot before facing her friend. "Probably October. As long as rain doesn't bother you."

"I think I'd rather be soggy than melting."

Siobhan chuckled. Her friend did have a point.

"Remind me again, why we're traipsing out here in this horrid heat?"

"State Fair." Texas has some of the most undervalued national parks in the country. If she wanted her photographic career to flourish at a level suitable to the Baron name, she needed some recognition. Winning a ribbon or two at the Texas State Fair would fit the bill. Animal and nature photos dominated the history of award winning photography, and the Texas parks had both in abundance.

Bridget unscrewed the cap on her warm water bottle and guzzled what was left inside. "You've got twenty, thirty minutes tops to get your prize photograph and then we're heading back to the hotel for a water refill." Bridget's mouth tipped up in the closest thing to a smile Siobhan had seen all day. "And a dip in the pool to cool off sounds pretty good too."

Once again, her friend had a good point. The heat was a tad oppressive this time of year. "Deal."

Now a true grin spread across Bridget's face.

Ten minutes later, Siobhan lowered her gaze along the precipice to one side and spotted the perfect shot. "There."

Bridget's gaze danced left and right, up and around. "There were?"

Leaning against a boulder, her arm outstretched, Siobhan pointed at the lone pink bloom thriving amongst the rocky side. "Right there. That flower."

When Bridget's gazed reached the end of Siobhan's finger and settled on the flower, a deep frown formed between her brows. "Doesn't look like much of a shot to me."

"Oh it will be." In her mind, Siobhan could see it now. She just had to get. "Closer."

"What?" Bridget inched forward, glanced at the drop only a few feet away, and eased back. "There has to be another... hey, be careful."

Standing at the very edge of the hillside, Siobhan tipped her head and her camera but there was no way she could get the angle she wanted. Blowing out a deep breath, she looked up. Even she didn't have the nerve to climb along the rocky edge to get closer. Maybe if she had the right equipment, but not barehanded. And then she spotted it. A lone tree up above.

"I don't like that look." Her hand shading her eyes, Bridget lifted her gaze upward. "What ever you're thinking, this is a bad...hey. Where are you going?"

Anxious to get her shot while the sunlight was behind her, Siobhan took off up the narrow path at a fast clip. "The tree."

"Tree?" Bridget followed, her attention on the rocky path. "Are you sure you Barons aren't part mountain goat. Slow down."

"I don't have much time."

"You have your whole life ahead of you. That is unless we fall off this cliff. Slow down."

"There." The lone tree stood strong and tall, if a little lifeless.

"What do you want with a dead tree?" Bridget inched left, avoiding the edge of the rocky path. There was no missing the moment Bridget's gaze shifted from the drop to her right, then back to Siobhan. A gasp could have been heard clear across the ravine. "Get off that tree."

Already halfway up the trunk, Siobhan was convinced the roots were firmly planted and even if there was little life left in the tree, all she needed was to reach that first limb and she'd be able to shimmy across for her shot.

"Siobhan Pegeen Baron get down here right this minute!" Stomping her foot hard on the ground, Bridget dropped her fisted hands on her hips. "You're going to get yourself killed for a stupid photograph."

"It's not stupid, and I'm not going to...oops." Her foot skidded away from the rough bark and feeling the tug of gravity against her well-rounded Irish derriere, Siobhan quickly hugged the tree with both arms.

"Oh, dear Lord. Your mother will never forgive me. You scoot back here right this minute!"

Siobhan didn't have to look down at her friend to know the woman was both spitting mad and terrified. Now that Siobhan was literally out on a limb, there was no point in turning back without the shot. Releasing one arm to move the camera still dangling from her neck, Siobhan shifted her weight more heavily onto the massive branch.

"You're not listening to me."

"Just another minute." Unable to balance both her weight and the camera, Siobhan set her favorite camera on the branch and with a little scooting forward, clicked away. A cloud rolled by, creating partial shade beside the flower and she clicked some more. Mother Nature was wonderful.

The photograph taken, convinced the blue ribbon would be hers with these shots, she just had one thing to figure out. How the heck was she going to get out of this tree without getting herself killed?

All Jack Preston needed was a few hours of shut eye and he'd be able to do more than sleep in his soup tonight. Undoing his bow tie, he shoved it in his pocket and undid the shirt button that had been choking him for hours. When he'd donned this penguin suit last night, he'd expected to be home, or at least in bed, long before sunrise. What he hadn't expected was an after party to end all after parties.

The last two hours felt like he'd been swept back in time to a mid century musical blockbuster. Seriously, not till last night had he ever seen an entire room of guests singing around a grand piano for hours except for in old movies. Dancing with every able bodied single female in attendance was nothing unusual, but doing so until the sun sparkled through the penthouse windows and Devlin Baron's maid served the surviving twenty or thirty guests breakfast was another first.

Somehow between chatting up a stacked blonde he'd hoped to set a few sparks off with, being roped into reliving his and Devlin's senior year performances in Godspell, and the most ridiculous game of charades that had everyone laughing till they cried, Connie Danner had caught him in a moment of weakness and sweet talked him into being her last minute plus one to a black tie wedding. Another, blasted wedding. Tonight. This last year he'd been to more weddings than he had in the previous decade. When Andrew Baron married, the core group of college buddies who thought nothing of zipping over to Monaco for a good yacht party on a moment's notice hadn't been seriously affected. By the time his best party buddy, Kyle, married and hung up his party hat, a domino affect of falling bachelors seemed to have started. The newest crop of most eligible bachelors weren't the same as his long time cohorts.

Less than ten minutes on the road and his phone sounded, his mother's name flashing on his dashboard. With a tap of his steering wheel, he picked up the call. "Hey, Mom."

"You're late."

Glancing quickly at the clock in front of him, he frowned forcing his mind to run through late for what.

"Margaret is muttering in the kitchen. You know how she hates keeping food warm."

Brunch. "Sorry, Mom. I'll be there in about fifteen minutes."

"See you then, son." The softness returned to her voice. "Love you."

"Love you too." No matter how tired he might be, his mom's routine of saying love you rather than goodbye, always made him smile.

At the next stop light, he rolled up his sleeves, undid another button on his shirt, and made a mental note to grab his loafers from the trunk and ditch the dress shoes. Even though he was no longer a teen needing to sneak around from his parents' oversight, he could at least try and not make it too obvious that he'd been out all night.

His phone dinged with a message as he pulled onto his family's property. The dashboard spit out that Connie needed to be at the church an hour early to dress with the girls, but her car was making funny noises on the drive home and would he please pick her up instead of meeting her there. Though he'd rather have had a few extra minutes to nap this afternoon, it looked like he was going to be hanging out in an empty church waiting for another wedding. Parked in front of the house, he tapped out *No Problem* and slipping the phone into his pocket, darted up the front steps.

Already seated at the table, his father casually let his gaze scan Jack from head to toe and back before a familiar deep set lines formed between his brows. "Late night?"

Jack resisted the urge to make excuses and simply dipped his chin before leaning over his mother's side for a quick hug and kiss hello. "Still playing bridge this afternoon?"

Smiling sweetly, his mother spread jam on a croissant and nodded. "The McKenzies are in Europe so we're playing with the Whitehalls. Should be interesting."

Serving himself from the buffet sideboard, he pulled up an image of the Whitehalls in his mind. "Isn't she the one who cheats at cards?"

"They both do," his father muttered over the coffee cup at his lips.

"We have a plan." His mother's grin turned sly. "We're going to insist the men play against the women. Tiffany won't have a partner to signal."

Jack smiled at his mother. The woman always had a solution for any problem.

"Speaking of partners." His father set his coffee cup down on the table. "You're not getting any younger."

And here came the familiar song and dance. Ever since Jack's thirty-fifth birthday, his father had been more insistent that it was time for him to settle down. Ever since Kyle's wedding, his father had found a way to work the subject into every, and any, conversation. "None of us are."

"You know what I mean." His father reached for a warm croissant and split it open. "Even Kyle Baron smartened up and found a nice wife. At this rate you're going to be wearing dentures and raising kids at the same time."

"No need to exaggerate Dad. I'm not that old."

"You're not that young either."

Touché. It wasn't like Jack didn't envy Kyle and his brothers just a little bit, but some men weren't cut out for settling down. Jack didn't have it in him to be domesticated. His father would simply have to accept sooner or later that watching TV with the little woman and changing diapers was not in the cards for Jack.

Read more of Just One Shot available now

MEET CHRIS

Author of over fifty contemporary novels, including the award winning Aloha Series, Chris Keniston lives in North Texas with her husband, two adult children, and two canine children. Though she loves her puppies equally, she admits being especially attached to her German Shepherd rescue. After all, even dogs deserve a happily ever after.

More on Chris and her books can be found at www.chris keniston.com.

Follow Chris on facebook at ChrisKenistonAuthor or on twitter @ckenistonauthor.

Join Chris' newsletter! Enjoy inside peeks from Chris' world and stories, receive notification of new releases, and sometimes she'll thank her subscribers with a free copy of a new 99 cent flirt.

Please, if you enjoyed reading Just One Taste, consider helping other readers find the Billionaire Barons of Texas Series by taking a moment to leave a review. Reviews are a blessing to authors and readers alike. Even just a few words will do! Thank you.

Printed in the USA
CPSIA information can be obtained
at www.ICGtesting.com
LVHW090259190124
769391LV00024B/385